PRAISE FOR BARRY UNSWORTH'S WORK

The Rage of the Vulture: "Superb storytelling. The richness of [Unsworth's] language and imagery shimmers on every page." —*Washington Post Book World*

"A novel of revelation . . . haunting." —*The New Yorker*

Stone Virgin: "A brilliant, ironic, sublime version of the Pygmalion legend." —*San Francisco Chronicle*

"No brief synopsis could suggest the sinuous intricacy of *Stone Virgin* or the adroitness with which Barry Unsworth manipulates the weighty mysteries of love, death, creation, faith, evil and the lure of history. . . . Consistently astonishing." —*Boston Globe*

Booker Prize–winning *Sacred Hunger*: "Utterly magnificent. . . . By its last page, you will be close to weeping." —*Washington Post*

"This brilliantly suspenseful period piece about the slave trade in the 18th century is also a masterly meditation on how avarice dehumanizes the oppressor as well as the oppressed." —*Chicago Tribune*'s "Outstanding Fiction"

"Quite possibly the best novel I've read in the last decade. . . . It is a completely satisfying literary experience and a great story, wonderfully told." —David Halberstam

Booker Prize–nominated *Morality Play*: "A learned, witty, satisfying entertainment. . . . Nicholas Barber seems too good a narrator to let go after just one short book." —*New York Times*

"Works brilliantly on three levels. It's an accurate, carefully imagined historical novel, set in 14th-century England; a dark and suspenseful murder mystery; and a provocative meditation on the birth of a new art form."
—Adam Begley, *Chicago Tribune*

After Hannibal: "Vivid, sinuous, profound, and entirely beguiling."
—Richard Eder, *Los Angeles Times Book Review*

"A brilliant novel, exquisitely precise in its analysis of evil twisting its way through ordinary lives."   —*Boston Globe*

Losing Nelson: "Exhilarating. . . . A pleasure, a puzzle, and a provocation."   —*New York Times Book Review*

"What a joy it is to have in hand a work of fiction that is at once thoroughly serious and—as all such fiction should be—immensely entertaining, in the deepest and best sense of the word."   —*Washington Post Book World*

THE BIG DAY

BOOKS BY BARRY UNSWORTH

The Partnership
The Greeks Have a Word for It
The Hide
Mooncranker's Gift
The Big Day
Pascali's Island
The Rage of the Vulture
Stone Virgin
Sugar and Rum
Sacred Hunger
Morality Play
After Hannibal
Losing Nelson

THE BIG DAY

BARRY UNSWORTH

W. W. Norton & Company
New York   London

ISBN 0-393-32149-5 pbk.

W. W. Norton & Company, Inc.
500 Fifth Avenue, New York, N.Y. 10110
www.wwnorton.com

W. W. Norton & Company Ltd.
Castle House, 75/76 Wells Street, London W1T 3QT

1 2 3 4 5 6 7 8 9 0

THE BIG DAY

1

On the morning of her fortieth birthday Lavinia woke earlier than usual. She lay in her room in the Regional College of Further Studies, of which her husband Donald was Founder and Principal, drowsing through the songs of birds from the garden below, feeling against her eyelids the strengthening light, thinking in a sleepy, sliding way about her fancydress party, only a few hours off now, and about the people she had invited, people she knew quite well, for the most part, but they would be transformed, unrecognizable, completely unpredictable in their costumes and masks. Nobody would know who anybody else was. That had been her idea, the beauty of her idea, from the start: a beauty which illumined her musings now. Nobody would know, until midnight. She had forbidden anyone to reveal what they were coming as, and masks were to be kept on till midnight. A real carnival party.

Morning light continued to seep in, reddened by its passage through Lavinia's ruby curtains. Though more or less awake now, she kept her eyes closed. It was strange to be forty. This warm heap of flesh that was herself in the bed had kept its blood moving somehow, and its nerves strung, for forty years. She felt vulnerable, this morning. Not fragile, but in need of careful handling, easily spilt. I am at my full, she thought. That is the way to put it. What I need is a man with steady hands. Immediately, by what seemed the action of some magnetic field in the mind, other attributes clustered around this primary one of steadiness: tall, erect carriage, thin but wiry, greying at the temples. A picture emerged of a randy, soldierly person. Such men existed – it was part of Lavinia's world-view that men to suit every need were perpetually circulating – but they were only to be found by romantic accident. They were certainly, she thought, not in the next bedroom, where her husband Donald lay, presumably still sleeping. Perhaps Mr Honeyball, who was coming to tea that afternoon . . . But he was not a steady man either. Indeed, it had been the glint of fanaticism in Mr Honeyball, the promise, beneath his rather mincing exterior, of a frenzy she hoped would prove sexual, that had first attracted her interest. She would learn more about that, she hoped, this afternoon . . .

Meanwhile, she suddenly recalled, as it was a Monday, she would have to go and see old Mrs Mercer at the Home, as usual. The fact that it was her birthday did not affect obligations of this kind. The old lady looked forward so to her visits. Besides, she would probably need to be reminded about the party. She was coming too, the only guest to be excused costume. It would be a treat for the old thing, Lavinia thought vaguely. Her guests in various disguises began passing in procession through her mind again, attempting to converse through their masks.

'Donald!' she called. 'Are you awake?'

There was no reply from the next room. Lavinia opened her eyes wide and stared up at the ceiling, still dark above the bed.

In the State Institution for the Aged, which Lavinia was to visit later that morning, many of the old folk were already up and about. Mrs Greenepad, extracting toast from her electric toaster at a few minutes before seven, heard on her radio forecasts of showers, some of them prolonged, and bright intervals. There was word also of an articulated vehicle wrecked across a motorway in the Midlands, causing inconvenience to motorists. Mrs Greenepad did not give this her full attention. At seventy-nine, though active still, she tended to regard all such happenings as outside her sphere. She listened assiduously to the news bulletins, not in quest of detailed information, but for the satisfaction of having her belief confirmed that total world collapse was just round the corner and that she might yet live to see it.

Noticing on the table margarine instead of butter, she directed a look of sharp reproof at the dishevelled back of Mrs Mercer's head. Mrs Mercer was her room-mate, and there was already some bad feeling between the old ladies, as Mrs Greenepad was jealous of Mrs Mercer's being invited to a fancy-dress party that evening. Now, with peculiar obstinacy, Edwina had again laid out margarine, instead of butter. It did not occur to Mrs Greenepad to replace the margarine with butter, nor quietly to lay butter alongside. She was keen to have the matter out with Edwina Mercer, once and for all, and was on the point of speaking when the pips for the seven o'clock news intervened. There were some vague introductory phrases, then a man's voice, rather jubilant in tone, said,

First the news headlines. The Prime Minister and leaders of the opposition parties will be meeting later today. No details have yet been published as to the agenda, but in the light of the worsening economic situation it is widely believed that the main purpose of the meeting will be to explore possibilities of forming a Government of National Unity. Most experts however, in view of the differences ... .

'Edwina,' Mrs Greenepad said. She was meaning to embark on the margarine question, but at that same moment Edwina turned her head and began speaking.

'What a lovely voice,' Edwina said, evidently referring to the news-reader. 'Hasn't he got a lovely voice?'

... now entering its third day with no immediate prospect of a breakthrough in the negotiations.

'That is a new voice,' Mrs Greenepad said. 'That man is a newcomer to the B.B.C.' It was her radio; Edwina only listened to it by her permission, and she felt herself to be an authority on all that it put forth. 'That is a young voice,' she said.

... struggling to mobilise both domestic and international support to combat famine conditions that it is feared may persist well into next year. The latest central government estimate of the number of starvation deaths in the past three months is thirty-two thousand, but other sources put the figures ...

'He will be one of the younger echelons,' Mrs Greenepad said. 'One of those they are training up.'

'Younger echelons?' Mrs Mercer looked straight before her, concentrating deeply, stealthily. They had announced the man's name, and it had been a name familiar to her. The prospect of catching Emily out made her quite forget the cramp in her left leg.

. . . speak of scenes of complete chaos and terror in the immediate aftermath of the explosion. Police and ambulance teams describe piercing cries from the wrecked interior as they dug in the rubble with bare hands in order to reach the victims. One eye-witness . . .

'Blythe,' Mrs Mercer said suddenly. She twisted her tangled head round so that she could watch Emily, get the maximum effect. 'His name is Blythe. He is an old hand at the studios; he has been a news-reader for a good many years now.'

Emily's face was too old and crumpled to give much away, but Edwina could tell by the agitated way her room-mate smoothed her palms down the front of her dress that the shot had gone home.

'Well, that is news to me,' Emily said, in an offended voice. 'You left the margarine out again,' she added, after a moment.

Edwina made no reply to this, merely raising to her eyes, which were discharging rather badly this morning, a small white cotton handkerchief. She dabbed at her eyes, watched over the border of her hanky Emily repeating that tell-tale gesture of the hands down the front of the dress.

'Donald!' Lavinia called again, looking up wide-eyed at the tremulous encroachments of light on the ceiling overhead. She thought, not for the first time, how nice it would be to have a large mirror, gilt framed to go with the rest of the décor, set in the ceiling over the bed, so that people could watch themselves. No good suggesting such a thing to Donald, of course – it would simply bring out all his latent conservatism. He was forward-looking in other ways; when it came to the School, for example, he had plenty of vision. He was fond of saving, and it was quite true, that he had built up the business out of nothing; but in sexual matters he showed no such initiative; he was a creature of habit. And lately, even that could not be depended on. Still, she thought, it is my birthday after all, so why not, and she called again, 'Donald, are you awake?'

Cuthbertson heard these calls, as he had heard the first, but he made no response. That morning, every morning for weeks now, he had awoken very early, before dawn, to a sensation of intense

4

fear. He had no defence against this, as it attacked him always before he was ready, before he had dressed, donned his glasses, summoned fortitude. It was a sense of danger acute but un-localized, like walking through long grass in which a beast lurked somewhere. Sky clear above, but every step attended with dread. To avoid snake bite or crocodile crunch the best thing to do is keep still, and Cuthbertson did his best to achieve perfect immobility. He lay there, quite still, and the day stretched before him, a perilous savannah.

He was lying on his back, hands rigidly down by his sides. He licked the dry roof of his mouth and his mind moved cautiously among memories. The past was dangerous too, but in a different way. Somewhere, at some point, he had taken a wrong step, made some ghastly mistake. He knew this, because it was the only way of explaining his present sufferings. If only he could be patient and painstaking enough he might locate that moment, and somehow nip, sterilize, douse it, before its consequences gathered and engulfed him. The effort required was great because to the normal labour of recollection was added the impossibility of knowing whether the moment had seemed other than commonplace at the time. He was not required to remember highlights only. No incident, however trivial, could be safely disregarded. At present he was thinking of a time twenty-two years and three months previously, when he had given Lavinia, to whom he was then engaged, a bunch of daffodils.

Daffodils, jonquils, narcissus. He checked, as always, the type of flower. Big, yes, and yellow all over, a more or less uniform yellow. Daffodils. Hyperbolical yellow in that white room. Clumsily untying the string or perhaps twine. The clumsiness was partly that and partly actually giving them, how to behave, what to say. What did I say? They were very yellow in that light. The bay below the hotel was a generator of white light, and the walls, the walls of the room were white. Her eyes filled with tears. I was trying to untie the string, twine. The stems were pale green, and they were thick, fleshy. The string, twine, cut the stems and some of it got on my hands, afterwards it turned brown. A brown stain. No, that was not daffodils, that was dandelions, that was years before. Where the stems were cut and bruised, the stems of the

5

dandelion, no, daffodil, this thin milky stuff came out. Sap? Her eyes filled with tears. She was regarding the daffodils in some way differently. What impulse led me to buy them? How can I ever know? Those brown stains, I was a child then, that was dandelion for the rabbits . . .

A terrible sense of having lost control assailed Cuthbertson. He tried to fight his way back to the white room, yellow flowers, Lavinia's face, but rabbits obtruded their faces, staring fastidiously through wire-mesh, he was a boy again, bare-kneed, cutting dandelion . . . He groaned, raising his head a little from the pillow, as if seeking help, or struggling to break through delirium. There was daylight in the room now. Each leaf and loop of the moulded wreath on his ceiling was visible. He raised his rigid left arm, bent it towards him, looked at his watch. It was eight minutes past seven.

. . . describe it as a scene in a nightmare, dismembered bodies lying on the pavement outside, people wandering about amid the wreckage in a state of shock, some of them bleeding from face wounds . . .

'Listen to the timbre of that man's voice,' Mrs Greenepad said. 'That is a young man's voice.' She compressed her mouth so that her thin bluish lips disappeared altogether, and stared inimically at Mrs Mercer. 'You put the margarine out again,' she said.

. . . situation in the interior is extremely grave. It now seems that even if supplies . . .

'You thought I wouldn't notice, didn't you? I can tell by the colour.'

. . . whole villages of dead and dying . . .

'You haven't got a weight problem, not like me.'

. . . lie out in the open, where dying mothers still try to feed babies too exhausted to . . .

'You haven't got a weight problem, Emily, that is what it is.' Mrs Mercer paused. Then with a sort of despairing effrontery, because Emily always proved stronger in the end, and because it was Emily's radio, she said, 'You are an old bag of bones, that is what *you* are.' Losing more nerve, she added quickly, 'Speaking from the medical viewpoint, not personal.'

'How dare you?' Mrs Greenepad said. 'Have you forgotten that it is my radio?'

'I am not likely to forget.'

'No,' Mrs Greenepad said. 'Nor are you likely to have a radio of your own.'

'Speaking in the medical sense,' Mrs Mercer said, 'and in that sense only, you are skin and bone, Emily.'

'Pronouncing his name to be Blythe. You cannot possibly be as conversant with the personnel as I am.'

. . . aged twenty, said that one of the soldiers ripped off her clothes and she was . . .

'Not like me. I've got a bit of flesh on me.'

. . . repeatedly . . .

'Such rudeness. I could cut you off from the source of your information, just like that.' Mrs Greenepad attempted in her rancour a snapping of the fingers, but succeeded in producing only a brief, dry, crepitant sound, 'How dare you make personal aspersions?' she said.

. . . tried to take a nine-month baby from one of the soldiers, saying she was its mother . . .

'And my hair the same colour it had when I was a girl.' Mrs Mercer's eyes were discharging badly again.

. . . The naked body of a young girl was found last night hidden in thickets near her Sunderland home . . .

'I'd be ashamed,' Mrs Greenepad said, 'if it was me. Appearing for breakfast in that state of dishabille.' She was referring to her room-mate's disordered hair, and the gaping front of her pale-blue candlewick dressing-gown.

'The same colour. Not like some. Even my worst enemies – '

'You wallow in it. Edwina, that is the only word. You ought to wear a girdle.'

. . . aged eight, had been sexually . . .

'– admit I have good legs, in every sense of that word.'

'You ought to confine yourself within stricter limits.'

Edwina Mercer dabbed at her eyes again. The pain had returned to her leg. 'I cannot help it,' she said, thinking of Mrs Cuthbertson's fancy-dress party, 'if some of us are more in demand than others.' She was conscious of her resources of defiance draining rapidly away. 'You know what you can do with your radio,' she said, with almost her last flicker.

... At Woolston in Buckinghamshire yesterday Henry Wilson ate six live frogs in seventy-one seconds to win fifteen pounds and the title of All England Live Frog Swallowing Champion.

'My goodness,' Edwina said. 'What a strong constitution.'

'Slut!' Mrs Greenepad shouted, losing control of herself completely at the sight of Edwina's mild round face, partially obscured by the dishevelled hair, listening with no apparent sense of gratitude to announcements about frogs on a radio not her own. 'I will report you to the council,' she shouted, 'for trying to attract the glances of workmen.'

Not like mine, Edwina thought, and she let the other's voice go over her head. Not like mine, which say what you like, is flesh and blood still, and my hair the colour it had when I was a young girl ...

... The frogs went down between mouthfuls of —

With trembling fingers Mrs Greenepad switched her radio off.

'Donald!' Lavinia called again, less tentatively now, for she had heard that groaning noise from her husband's room.

Cuthbertson sighed heavily, clambered out of bed, padded over three yards or so of carpet and, still in the grip of the anguish that had woken him, opened the door to his wife's room. He stood for a moment, looking in warily, a pale, bulky man in dark blue pyjamas. Sensing the nature of this summons he had not bothered to put his glasses on, and so things were rather indistinct in his wife's room. However, the sweet synthetic odours of her existence came wafting to him.

'Come and get in beside me,' he heard her husky voice say.

'Happy birthday,' he said, suddenly remembering. He moved obediently towards the bed, feeling under his bare feet the alien luxury of her carpeting, so much thicker than his own. He got into the bed, sank down beside her. She turned to him, and he laid hands on her abundant, sleep-heavy breasts. Ritual endearment and caress, however, effected no change in him, none whatsoever. He lay heavy and tense beside her, and Lavinia, who knew nothing of his morning fears, began quite soon to reproach him, first for lack of ardour, an old grievance;

8

then for his unwillingness to experiment.

'A man of your experience,' she said, 'I should have thought . . .'

Cuthbertson failed to hear the next few words, then he heard 'variations'. He could not make out what his wife was talking about. He could not make out what he was doing, thus recumbent beside her. His mind was confused among yellow flowers, the oozing roots of daffodils, rabbits' nervous ears and noses.

'Different and exciting things to do,' Lavinia said, with sudden distinctness.

Cuthbertson made non-committal noises. He felt like a member of the audience who has been called upon to assist without knowing how the trick is done. The string, twine. That little bay an aimer of sea light . . .

'Thirty-six positions,' she said '*At least*. And we go on in the same old way.'

'Dispossessions?' he said. This word, which he thought she had said, chimed in with one of his current anxieties, one which had been deepened by a person named Honeyball, an official at the Ministry of Education, who had been a frequent visitor lately, and who hinted constantly at a State take-over. 'No fear of that,' he said, with assumed confidence. Suddenly, in some remote recess he felt intimidations of sexual excitement, but these faded almost at once, to be replaced by anxious thoughts about Mafferty, a member of staff recently appointed, who was proving unsatisfactory.

'Would you like to try it from behind?' Lavinia said, in the tone of one offering biscuits.

'From behind? No, I don't think so.' Dishevelled, unpunctual, smelling of drink, that was the count against Mafferty. He was to be interviewed that morning.

Raising himself a little and turning his wrist at the side of Lavinia's head, Cuthbertson checked the time: it was eighteen minutes past seven. Mafferty was to be interviewed in . . . three hours and twenty-seven minutes precisely. He had found it increasingly necessary of late to keep times firmly fixed in his head, otherwise the day slid away, lost form.

'Thank you all the same,' he said, with absent-minded politeness. Suddenly, and with irrepressible pride, he was aware of the

9

quiet house all about him, with its many rooms, hushed and prepared for the students; the gardens beyond neat borders, clipped hedges, straight alleys of shrubs. Himself at the centre. But not as he should be, not in masterful repose. It was as if the centre was sticky somehow, and held him, faintly twitching . . . The feeling of being in the toils of something began to descend on Cuthbertson, and with it some return of the fear that woke him daily, the terrible need for circumspection.

'Perhaps,' Lavinia said, with a sort of muffled, gloomy sarcasm, 'perhaps you would like to wear my clothes? My knickers, for example.'

'I don't think you ought to refer to them in that way,' Cuthbertson said, his hearing again affected. 'It could give offence.'

'Any way you like.'

'Blacks would be a better term. In my line of business I come across a good number.'

'Do you indeed? Well, if that is the colour you like best – '

'No, no,' Cuthbertson said, 'I have a great deal of sympathy for Africans, as for all emergent peoples, but I prefer my own pigmentation, basically.'

'What are you talking about, Donald? I asked you if you would like to wear my knickers.'

'*Knickers?*' Cuthbertson was silent for some moments, then he said slowly. 'No, I don't think so.' These suggestions, coming from so close beside him, were beginning to seem strangely like promptings from his own lower nature. He raised himself slightly and looked at his wife's face. Her large blue eyse regarded him unblinkingly. 'I thought you were comparing me with negroes,' he said. Suddenly he was stricken by doubts as to whether he had remembered to instruct Bishop, his Senior Tutor and Administrative Officer, to post up the examination results. No one who had paid the fee ever failed, of course, if conduct had been satisfactory, but it was vitally important to keep to the forms . . .

'What about a mirror in the ceiling?' Lavinia said.

Feverishly Cuthbertson sought in his mind among the mass of directives, notes, memoranda he had issued in the last few days. He could remember nothing relating to examination results.

'In a gilt frame,' Lavinia said, 'Who would you like to do it with?'

'I don't follow you.'

'If it wasn't me, who would you like to be doing it with?'

'You are the only – '

'Yes, but who, *who*?'

'Miss Naylor,' Cuthbertson said at random.

There was a short silence. Miss Naylor was his secretary. She was young, only twenty, and she had a very beautiful figure.

'No, no,' Lavinia said judiciously. 'Do it with Mrs Binks.' Mrs Binks, the wife of a member of his staff, was in her fifties and had a grim, large-jawed face, and a baying, rather blood-curdling laugh. The thought of sexual congress with Mrs Binks was not attractive to Cuthbertson.

'I don't really think – ' he began.

'Mrs Binks, Mrs Binks,' Lavinia said, '*Mrs Binks.*'

'Very well, my dear,' Cuthbertson said hollowly. 'Mrs Binks let it be.'

Lavinia waited some moments, as if to let thoughts of an unclothed Mrs Binks do their work. Then, as he made no further movement, uttered no futher sound, she sat up a little in the bed and turned her head accusingly towards him. 'You really are hopeless, Donald,' she said. 'I don't know how long we can go on like this.'

'I am sorry,' Cuthbertson said. He felt very little emotion, however, only a kind of generalized anxiety. He was aware of potential for sorrow deep within, but there was a thick wadding or padding around it, made up of all the things he had to worry about. His thoughts returned now to Mr Honeyball, and the threat of being taken over by the State.

'You ought to read the Karma Sutra,' Lavinia said.

'Mr Honeyball is coming to tea this afternoon, isn't he?' Cuthbertson said. 'Be nice to him, won't you? I believe he has a good deal of influence.'

This Honeyball, who occupied a place in the thoughts of both Donald and Lavinia, was at this moment making a confidential report to a man named Baines. They were sitting in the small,

II

meagrely furnished bed-sitting room rented by Baines on a weekly basis. Honeyball spoke rather quickly, not opening his lips very wide, not looking often at Baines, referring from time to time to a small pocket-book. He had called on his way to work, as he did Mondays and Thursdays, when Baines was in town. Any oftener than this, Baines thought, might be regarded as suspicious. Mr Honeyball was an official of the local branch of the Ministry of Education, in the Inspectorate Department, whose offices were in the centre of town.

The room was small and airless, with one narrow window looking out on to a blank wall. Baines was sitting at the table, before him a newspaper and an empty white plate. He was wearing dark blue pyjamas and a voluminous, tawny-coloured dressing-gown, which had moulted here and there, giving him a mangy look. However, he wore it with considerable style. He had tied a blue, polka-dotted cravat round his thick neck, and from his breast pocket there protruded a careless brown silk handkerchief. He kept his large, blue-featured face turned steadily towards Honeyball all the time the latter was speaking. When the report was finished there was silence for a while, with Honeyball looking modestly down at his sharply creased trousers, and Baines appearing to meditate.

'Is Kenneth getting the best of everything?' Baines said at last. His voice was deep, deliberate, curiously plangent, as if produced in an atmosphere different from that of his hearer. He was glancing, as he spoke, at the front page of his newspaper, at a picture of carnage and devastation, uniformed persons picking their way. Another bomb. Strange, he thought, perhaps a good omen, on this day of all days, when the Party was to explode its own smaller, obscurer bomb in the town, that there should be this national focus of outrage and indignation. The Party, of course, was aiming at property, not human lives. Not like these anarchist shits . . . Though listening to his underling Honeyball with a composed face, Baines felt exhilaration gathering deep within him at this patch of chaos in the newspaper, portent of that universal chaos they were aiming at, working for, in which amid blood and debris nations wheel and reform, from which all great cleansing, purifying movements are launched, the womb of –

He checked these thoughts, out of the long habit of conspiracy, and stared suspiciously at Honeyball, who knew nothing about the bomb plans.

'– been to see him in hospital,' Honeyball was saying. 'He seemed all right. He can't talk very well.' Aware of Baines' scrutiny, he moved his slender neck inside its restricting collar, in a restless movement habitual to him. Then Baines averted his face, and Honeyball was looking with awe at the profile of a Regional Controller, one of the Party's full-time officials.

'His face is still bandaged, of course,' he said. Kenneth had suffered a formidable blow in a street fracas two nights previously, when his nose and jaw had been broken.

'Has he any idea who did it?'

'None at all. He was with three others. They had succeeded in pulling the speaker down from his box, but then some people got in the way. Some of his own people I think. He did get hurt, actually. The speaker I mean. Ronald saw him being kicked. But it wasn't one of our men – it happened before they could get to him. It was late in the evening, you know, and several of the people in the crowd were drunk.' Honeyball paused, thinning his lips with distaste at this animality.

'You say the speaker is known to us?'

'Yes. He lives here in the town. It is the W.F.S., you know. Workers for a Free Society. Local branch.'

'Trotskyite scum,' Baines said mildly. 'Semites not far to seek there, old boy. Don't be taken in by this local branch jargon. They've got no national organization to speak of. I doubt if they could muster a hundred members.'

'Not like us,' Honeyball said, with immediate contempt for such weakness.

'Our strength is in the public, in public support and sympathy,' Baines said. He stood up, a tall, broad-shouldered, imposing figure, despite the mangy dressing-gown. 'We are not politicians,' he said. 'We are old-fashioned patriots. And that is not such a rare breed as these anarchist shits try to make out. There are millions of us, typical, inarticulate English men and women, waiting for someone to give them a lead, voice their deepest feelings. They can see what is happening to this country, Honeyball, and they are waiting. That patience, that courage, it still exists, Honeyball, in the bosoms of countless men and women throughout this country. Those are the things that made us great.'

'Hear, hear,' Honeyball said.

'When we have finished our game of bowls,' Baines said, 'we shall deal with these people who are trying to bring this country to its knees, and the reckoning will be heavy. It sounds like a loaded stick that was used on Kenneth. Something that was laid right across his face.'

'It does sound like that, yes.'

'He shall have a citation,' Baines said. 'As soon as he is sufficiently recovered. I will see to it personally. Here would probably be the best place for the ceremony. A simple bar, you know, for gallantry in the face of the enemy. For the moment, of course, it is merely a token, but one day, and that day is coming sooner than a lot of people think, our boys will be able to wear their insignia publicly and with pride. Tell him, will you?'

'I will, yes.' Honeyball felt a deep pang of jealousy and hostility towards Kenneth, now so contemptibly weak and disabled. His position as Branch Secretary precluded front line activities on his part.

'Wait a minute,' Baines said. 'I'll tell him myself. I think I can get along to the hospital later on this morning.' He paused for a moment or two, considering. He thought of the little brown bag under his bed. He had things to arrange today which had to be kept very quiet – even from the local party membership, and that included Honeyball. Besides, he hated hospitals and all evidence of sickness. 'Yes,' he said. 'I think I can fit it in. There is this wretched costume to hire, too, isn't there?'

'For Mrs Cuthbertson's party. Yes, that's right.'

'Well,' Baines said, 'it's got to be done, I suppose. You will take care of those papers, won't you? The Contingency Plans.'

'Yes, of course. They are safe in my brief-case. As soon as I get home tonight I'll put them under lock and key.'

'Good man. Absolutely fatal if they got into the wrong hands. It's not so much our own people, but various other groups – small concerns, but they are important collectively. Lots of little armies, you might say. Some more military than others, of course. Some not military at all. They must be kept in a state of resentment, Honeyball. At present it is the only unity they possess. That is the thinking up at Head-quarters and I think it is sound thinking.'

'So do I.'

'Good man. Well, as I say, it would be fatal to let the Press, for example, get hold of them. There are no names mentioned, but these are fairly detailed plans of what might be done, on a local basis, in the event of a breakdown, should the government prove ineffective.' Baines paused a moment, smiling. 'And it will,' he said. 'It will prove ineffective.'

'I know it will.'

'Good man. Well, it would reveal the political involvement, you see. I mean, all these people, there is no ideology in common, we must provide that, but they would be ready to act if things got to a certain stage . . . That is what we need, that sort of vigilante spirit, but not identified with a party . . .'

'That would come later.' Honeyball said, with a little, coughing laugh.

'Exactly,' Baines said. 'Well, I suppose I'd better start getting dressed.'

'I'll be on my way then,' Honeyball said, looking modestly aside.

'You have some time left, haven't you?'

Honeyball looked at his watch. 'Yes,' he said. 'It is only seven-thirty.'

'I thought we might have a talk about this Cuthbertson chap,' Baines said.

Without his glasses Cuthbertson couldn't see the farther reaches of his wife's room very clearly. The dressing-table and the clutter of objects upon it were indistinct, as was the large white and gilt wardrobe nearby. The brown and gold pansies on the wallpaper ran together.

He rose, and padded softly back over the thick carpet to his own room. Once there, he went to his bedside table, found his glasses and put them on. At once the blurred world resettled into clear images. The house took shape around him, assumed the day's business and purposes. His own room, as always, pleased him by its order and simplicity: single, iron-framed bed, plain oak chest of drawers, narrow wardrobe, white-shaded lamp. Standing there, looking round, Cuthbertson, strove to reassure himself by an elementary process of logic: this room, of which I am the owner, demonstrates beyond doubt its owner's competence and control . . . Everything is all right, he thought. It is perfectly obvious that everything is all right. Why do I worry about lists, about persons like Honeyball and Mafferty? Everything emanates from me. In my capacity as Principal *I cannot be wrong*. Every directive issuing from me is at once transformed into the corporate reality of the School . . .

Almost at once, however, even as he was reaching for his dressing-gown behind the door, he experienced a fresh wave of panic. He had suddenly remembered that today was Degree Day. This ceremony took place every six weeks and was an important and colourful occasion. His fear was due to the fact that only now, when he had been awake several hours, had it come into his mind. He had been in danger, therefore, all this time, of forgetting it completely . . . In an attempt to steady himself he began to utter incantatory phrases in his mind. It falls to my lot . . . It must surely be apparent to you all . . . If that is the general feeling of the meeting . . . Far be it from me . . .

This worked, as it sometimes did, and after a moment or two he was able to go back to the door and look in on his wife again. She had hoisted the pillow up, thus raising the angle of her head. He saw her face and met her eyes. For a moment or two they regarded each other in silence and to each of them during those moments the other seemed curiously typical: Lavinia with the flush of her excitement still lingering on her broad, fair-browed, guileless-looking face, at home in this room, her natural habitat, where shades of pink and brown struggled for supremacy, where almost everything was fringed or frilled, from shocking pink lamp shade to brown velvet cushions; and he with that sad doggedness, head up and shoulders braced, after his lamentable failure, thick dark eyebrows above horn-rimmed glasses, the heavy body and the heavy face.

'I don't know how long we can go on like this, Donald,' she said. 'You won't seek advice.'

Cuthbertson walked to the bed, one hand going to his dressing-gown pocket. The simple pleasure of being about to give Lavinia something excluded everything else from his mind. 'This is for you,' he said. 'A token of my – '

The pocket, however, was empty. His fingers curled softly, unbelievingly round in it.

'A small gift,' he said, thrusting his hand hastily into the other pocket. There was nothing there, either. 'I trust that over the years,' he said, his desire to make a speech surviving the shock by a few seconds. Then he stopped. 'But I . . . It must be . . .' he said. He felt his knees begin to tremble. Panic again threatened, and he fought against it, opening his mouth and taking deep breaths. 'My God,' he said. He strove to remember himself actually putting the jewel box there, but could recall only the luminous intention, and the shape and glisten of the locket itself, in his hand. He had taken it out to look at it, yes. But in that case . . . 'My God,' he said again, appalled at his inability to remember.

'Are you feeling all right, Donald?'

Through a mist he saw Lavinia sitting up in bed, regarding him alertly. Caution came to him, the need for concealment.

'Silly of me,' he said, twitching his mouth into a smile. 'I had something for you. I must have . . .'

'You probably left it downstairs somewhere,' she said. 'Never mind, it will be something to look forward to. Don't tell me what it is, will you? I'd like it to be a surprise.'

'All right,' he said.

'You are silly, Donald.'

'I suppose I am,' Cuthbertson said, normal speech miraculously continuing to proceed from him in spite of the sickening chaos this miscarriage of plan had thrown his mind into.

'You should not be so set in your ways,' she said. 'There are books, manuals, which give details.'

'I beg your pardon?' Cuthbertson said.

'Take the Karma Sutra, for example.'

Suddenly he realized that she had reverted to the former topic. 'The Karma Sutra?' he said. 'Do you really expect me, at my time of life, to imitate natives?' The sense of outrage cleared his mind. The rhetorical impulse, always strong in him, became imperious.

The moment to assert himself had arrived. 'Of all the ways,' he began, in commanding tones, and then paused, looking down at her, marshalling his thoughts.

'You could take a leaf out of their book,' Lavinia said.

'Distinguishing human beings, I say of all the ways distinguishing human beings from the . . . from animals, the rest of the animal kingdom, let me put it that way . . .'

'More than one, several,' Lavinia said.

'No, no,' Cuthbertson said, loudly and vehemently. 'It is in the methods in connexion with copulation, copulatory methods, to put it . . . Therein lies the distinguishing feature. Human beings make love face to face. Lavinia, we have developed a frontal style.'

He stood for a moment, head up, shoulders squared, seeking the question to end on. Now he had it. 'Why should we turn, for models, to lower forms in the evolutionary train?'

'Human to drink water,' Lavinia said. 'From the clear spring. But it doesn't put us among the beasts to have a shandy now and again.'

'I'm going to have my bath,' Cuthbertson said, offended that Lavinia had not seen the superior quality of his arguments. He turned and retreated rapidly into his own room, passed straight through it without pausing, and went out into the corridor. 'Sherry, brandy, beer,' he heard Lavinia's voice calling after him.

He made his way to the bathroom with a sense almost of being pursued. He locked himself in and put on the cold shower, letting it run cold while he undressed. Before getting under he regarded his blanched corpulence for some seconds in the long mirror set in the wall, inspected his tongue and eyeballs, the paucity of hair on his crown. The thin spray of the shower looked like steam almost, but he could feel the chill of it. He nerved himself to get under, endure the doubt-expelling, fear-expelling, shock. It was the only thing, he had found, in the morning, which would settle his mind. He had not missed a morning now for . . . five months and ten days. Shivering in his nakedness he checked and double-checked this calculation. Yes, absolutely right. The reassuring sense of exactitude, mastery of brute fact, enabled him once again to achieve the matutinal self-conquest. He stepped under the shower. Enclosed within a plastic screen he writhed and clutched.

Baines had taken off his dressing-gown and his pyjama jacket, and now stood for some moments fronting Honeyball. The skin of his body was very pale. Light auburn hair formed a cross on it, the vertical bar reaching down to the top of his pyjamas. His shoulders were smooth, heavy, with a pronounced slope. 'Now what about this Cuthbertson chap?' he said.

Honeyball looked timidly at his chief's naked torso. 'I have been there twice since I saw you last,' he said. 'You are going to the party tonight then?'

'This fancy dress affair?' Baines turned to the chair on which his clothes were draped, picked up the pale pink shirt, and looked closely at the collar. 'Yes,' he said. 'I think it is important for us both to go. I have hopes of these Cuthbertson people. You don't see a pair of cuff-links, do you, up there on the mantelpiece?'

'Yes,' Honeyball said. 'Here they are. Can I put them in for you?'

Baines smiled. His eyes had a way of widening when he smiled, which gave his face an appearance of great charm. 'If you like,' he said, extending an arm. 'You are a good fellow, Honeyball. Your value is known at Headquarters, believe me.'

The smile vanished, however, as he found himself looking down from close quarters at Honeyball's narrow, neat, saurian head. Not a pure type, Honeyball. 'The day is coming,' Baines said, 'and coming sooner than a lot of people think, when we shall be able to fulfil our natures, be ourselves, play the roles we were intended for.'

'Certainly,' Honeyball said.

'In the meantime, Honeyball, it is all a subterfuge. We are dressed in borrowed robes, to quote the bard. You're going there this afternoon, aren't you?

'To the School? Yes.' Honeyball lowered his head, increased his concentration. He was normally very nimble with his fingers, but the Regional Controller's nearness was making him clumsy.

'Good man. Finished that one?' Baines extended his other arm.

'She has asked me to tea again. I don't quite know why. It is the second time in the last week. Perhaps she wants to pass on some message from him, from Cuthbertson.'

'Mysterious lady,' Baines said jovially. 'Why has she invited me to her party, for that matter? She doesn't know me.'

'I spoke to her about you.'

'I hope you didn't say too much,' Baines said, with a sudden change of tone.

'I spoke of you as a friend.' Honeyball, who had registered this change, did not dare look up as he said this. He had once seen Baines seriously displeased, and it had frightened him. He heard Baines breathing above him, passed a few moments of half-pleasurable apprehension, then after a moment the voice, restored to joviality, said, 'Good man. You're a bit of a butterfingers, aren't you?'

'Not as a rule,' Honeyball said. 'There, it's finished now.'

'You have been working on Cuthbertson?'

'Yes. I have been going on in the way we decided. He now quite definitely believes that my position in the Ministry gives me access to inside information about take-over plans and so forth. I think he also believes, though he pretends not to, that there is a possibility of the State extending its ownership over all the places of further education. Either that, or if they cannot be made to fit into any official category, closing them down altogether. And not only that.' Honeyball smiled. His teeth were small, neat, yellowish. 'He is actually coming round to the belief that I can influence the decision, on a local basis.' His smile widened. 'He is gullible,' he said, 'for a man in his position.'

'Everyone is gullible these days,' Baines said, 'It comes from the sense of crisis. Disaster makes people gullible, Honeyball. And it suits our book very well. It suits us as far as Cuthbertson is concerned, and it suits us generally. The readiness to believe in what we are trying to create. The readiness of the State to purify itself. Any means of achieving that readiness is justified. Ripeness is all, to quote the bard. You can't see a pair of black shoes over there, can you? Over near the bed?'

'I'll have a look.' Honeyball went in the direction indicated. 'No,' he said, after a moment. 'I can't see any shoes here.'

'Perhaps they got pushed under the bed,' Baines suggested.

'Here they are,' Honeyball said, on hands and knees beside the bed. 'They need a bit of a wipe-over. Can I do it for you?'

'By all means. You'll find some polish and a brush at the bottom of the cupboard.' Baines removed his pyjama trousers and threw them on to the bed. His legs were rather short in relation to his body, and thickly covered with glinting gingerish hair. 'What we need,' he said, 'and I know I have said this before, is a room in that house of theirs, a rent-free office in that building. He must have rooms he doesn't use. It would be marvellous cover. Do you think he can be persuaded?

'I think he might be,' Honeyball said, busy with the shoes.

'That is our first objective, Honeyball. A base, a foothold, a room in that house. But there is more at stake than that. If these people could be made . . . sympathetic to our cause, think of it, Honeyball. Think of it in terms of possible donations. Money is not plentiful up at Headquarters, you know.'

'I know it,' Honeyball said.

'And Cuthbertson must be quite rich.'

'Very rich, yes.'

'It is important that he should be handled in the right way. I want you to keep this to yourself, Honeyball, but the people up at Headquarters have decided that this is what is officially known as a High Potential Area. It is predominantly middle and lower-middle. Very little industry as such, and relatively small proletariat. Large number of chronically insecure small businessmen and self-employed persons. Out towards the coast a lot of people on fixed incomes with inflation going up. Then there is the military base, all those trainee officers, and the Government threatening further defence cuts. It has all the ingredients, Honeyball.'

'I see that, yes.'

Baines began to put his grey flannel trousers on. 'Which means,' he said, 'that they will be watching developments here with particular interest. By the way, what is *she* like?'

'Mrs Cuthbertson?' Honeyball blushed a little. 'She doesn't seem to care about the school, as such,' he said.

Baines, noting the blush, laughed in a barking way. 'Got her mind on other things, has she?' he said. 'Well, you must be ready, aye ready, Honeyball. No sacrifice is too great.'

Honeyball's blush deepened. He looked down. 'Your shoes are ready, Eric,' he said.

'Thank you.' Baines looked at his servitor in silence for some moments. Not really enough panache there to exploit a situation like this, he thought. He had a shrewd suspicion that Honeyball, at thirty-five, was still a virgin. Perhaps just as well he was to meet her himself. He had always been a great one for the ladies. God bless the ladies, he often said to himself and others. Where should we be without them? 'Do you think Cuthbertson worries about being shut down on legal grounds?' he said. 'He must be sailing near the wind, dishing out his own degrees like that.'

'As the law is constituted at present there's nothing illegal in it. Anyone can open a school and charge what fees and run what courses he likes. He can issue his own certificates, diplomas, degrees. There are a good number of such places up and down the country.'

'Parasites,' Baines said. 'Their days are numbered, old boy.'

'What makes Cuthbertson unusual is that he actually runs the place as a school, employs teachers, and so forth. I mean, most of these places do it by post; you take a very expensive course of correspondence lessons and you get your degree. But Cuthbertson insists on giving value for money, as he would probably put it. He has a sort of ethical attitude towards it. No one gets a degree who hasn't attended. He is an idealist, in his way.'

'He is a crook, in his way, too,' Baines said. 'It is foreigners he mostly attracts, isn't it? Back home in Abu Dhabi people won't know the difference, that's the idea, isn't it?'

'Partly. But he gets quite a few English people too. People who want to be able to say they've got a degree. People who want to get jobs in undeveloped countries.'

'Knaves and fools, that's what it comes down to. I don't call a man like that an idealist.'

'I only meant that in his own eyes he is a man of principle.'

'*We* are idealists,' Baines said, and Honeyball realised from his manner that he had been offended by the application of this word to Cuthbertson.

'Working in poverty and obscurity,' Baines said, 'to make this country great again.'

'True,' Honeyball said. 'It was the wrong word.'

'Still, if he is confused about his motives, so much the better for us. He will be more suggestible.'

22

Baines mused for a moment. Dressed now in his flannel trousers and navy-blue, double-breasted blazer, he looked large, handsome, dependable. 'We are desperately short of funds,' he said. 'You know that. If we could estblish some sort of influence there, it would be invaluable. And highly regarded at top level. It is just the sort set-up I regard as promising. A basically crooked enterprise, whatever the law says, and whatever the illusions of this Cuthbertson chap.'

He began to pace backwards and forwards in front of Honeyball. 'I can smell it,' he said. 'Money is of first importance to us just now. Every penny of expenditure is carefully scrutinized up there, Honeyball. Even the cost of hiring a costume for this party tonight will have to be accounted for. I myself live on a pittance. Not because they are niggardly – there are some very noble natures up there. It is simply that money is so short. These Cuthbertsons sound the likeliest sources I've come across in ages. Believe me, I have a nose for these things.'

'I know you have,' Honeyball said, watching the pacing figure with awe and admiration.

'So keep at it, there's a good chap. You will be mentioned in despatches, never fear. Well, I won't keep you any longer now.'

The two men raised clenched fists and looked fixedly at each other for a moment. Then Honeyball, grasping his brief-case firmly, turned to the door.

'What are you going as, by the way?' Baines said.

'I'm going as Toad of Toad Hall,' Honeyball said. 'It is the only fancy dress outfit that I possess. There is a headpiece, you see, so I shan't need to bother about a mask.

'Good man.' Baines nodded his head approvingly.

When Honeyball had gone, he sat down again at the table, and looked at the newspaper. Again the picture of debris and bodies on the front page drew his attention. Martyrs, they were martyrs. Even though they had died in ignorance. Probably left-wing terrorist shits who had planted the bomb. But it made no difference, no difference at all. This bomb, this damage, these deaths of men, women, children all helped towards that readiness he had spoken of earlier, to be achieved through the erosion of security. Millions of people would be horrified by this picture, this morning and some of their faith in government to enforce and protect would go.

The sight of the anonymous corpses stirred Baines: he was moved by the sacrifice. To have died like this was virtuous, it was to have played a part, however humble, in the dynamics of history. Their bodies would sprout flowers. There was almost a lump in his throat. He stood up abruptly, to break this unmanly weakness, and began striding back and forth across the worn carpet of the room. The life of the individual was as nothing. A collective grave, a mound humped with flowers. A moment before quick with life, instinct with beauty. Now anonymous meat. But not futile, no – those who directed history, those with the power and the wisdom to accept the violence necessarily inherent in the dialectical process, we know how important, how profoundly important . . . otherwise animals, clinging to life. A ground-swell of music began in his mind, building up to a mighty surge, taking in on its sweep all the devastation, the wounds of the world, and bearing on in triumph.

2

It is now known, said Mrs Greenepad's radio, *that twenty-three people died and more than seventy were injured, many of them seriously, in the series of bomb outrages which took place yesterday evening.*

It was the eight o'clock news, and Mrs Greenepad was not giving it her whole attention, because she was listening for her room-mate's return from the bathroom. As soon as Edwina set foot inside the door, Mrs Greenepad was going to turn the set off.

Flying glass caused extensive facial injuries and it is feared that at least two . . .

That'll teach her, Mrs Greenepad thought, with vindictive pleasure. Setting up her contrary opinions. Putting on airs because she is invited out to a fancy-dress party. Anyone would think it was her radio. This Mrs Cuthbertson needs her head examined, inviting such a class of person, but she is not up to all that much herself, flighty creature, mutton dressed up as lamb, if you ask me . . .

Terrorist groups have already claimed responsibility for the explosions. The one thought most probable . . .

At this point, seeing Mrs Mercer's head appear round the door, and waiting only long enough for her room-mate to appreciate the significance of her action, Mrs Greenepad switched the set off.

Lavinia, unwitting cause of all this trouble, was still in bed. For some time after her husband had left the room, the names of drinks had continued to pass in desultory fashion through her mind. Gin and orange, gin and tonic, gin and It . . . Gin first and It afterwards, she thought, recalling a remark made by a lady in a pub years and years ago. Lady in a sheepskin jacket. I was shocked, she thought proudly. Take more than that to shock me now. Cherry brandy. Vodka. Mark of a barbarous person or a child always to want home cooking. How would mankind progress? Donald is a barbarous person. Bloody Mary, there's another one. Or perhaps a child. Making speeches at me . . .

She heard the bathroom door being locked and thought with wonder of Donald writhing under the cold shower. Part of the business of getting a grip, she thought vaguely. That was a favourite phrase of his. He was always girding himself up, while she herself drifted. Now, I am forty, she thought. My fortieth birthday will mark a turning-point. No one knew it was her birthday – no one but Donald. She had privately decided that this fancy-dress party was going to mark a turning-point, usher in a new era – she believed firmly in the possibility of Beginning Life Anew. There was no earthly reason, of course, why she should wait even that long for a new experience. Mr Honeyball was coming to tea that very afternoon and something might well emerge from that.

I have tried to broaden his outlook, she told herself, reverting to Donald, but he will not stretch himself. In any sense of that term . . . How his face changed, when he could not find whatever it was. Something small. Jewellery? and then he started day dreaming, right in the middle of our conversation. These days it happened more and more frequently that Donald lost the thread of things. He seemed somehow disabled by thoughts.

She tried for some moments to trace this behaviour to some definite beginning, some origin in an actual event. But it was impossible now even to be sure when she had first noticed it. Probably, she thought vaguely, Donald needed a holiday. He had hardly been away from the School in the last five years. Nor had she, for that matter. All the money the School was making, thousands and thousands, and what did they get out of it?

This last thought, of her own deprivations, broke her mood of vaguely affectionate concern about Donald, and she began to feel a sense of grievance. He had been dishonest, she confusedly felt, dishonest to argue, after his abysmal failure to honour her birthday, about *homo sapiens* being face to face. That wasn't the point at all, it wasn't just technical at all. She didn't care about positions really, and Donald knew that. The fact was, he didn't seem to want her any more.

Am I to be regarded as a mere adjunct to this School? she asked herself, and with the question thoughts of Mr Honeyball returned. He was so slim, and potentially, she hoped, vicious, owing to pent-up desire, with that thin moustache, narrow, rather peering grey eyes, frail-boned, snapping jaws. Though for the time being rather shy. She had made definite progress, she felt, on the last occasion, four days previously, when he had come to tea. That sleeveless Italian blouse had been effective, though rather chilly. He had gripped his cup with both hands, as if it might be blown away, and talked rapidly and at some length about that friend of his, of whom he seemed to have a high opinion, Baines, Eric Baines. He was coming to her party too . . . Hands that held on to things. What was the word? Prehensile. Rather military looking, Mr Honeyball, apart from this tendency of the hands to clutch. She must remember to ask him if he had served in the Forces. Shiny shoes, and always neat, and he kept his handkerchief in his sleeve, which she had always thought of as a military foible . . .

What would he come as? she wondered. He would make a good colonial officer, in a solar topee, pale and reduced by fever, in a high state of sexual tension, inflexibly set on doing his duty. With Mr Honeyball and his friend there were twenty-six people coming. Once again she began checking through the guests, experiencing that complex blend of excitement and foreboding. She herself was going as Venus, newly risen from the wave, decked in what she hoped would pass as foam . . . The urgency of these thoughts made her restless. It was time to be getting out of bed.

Since early girlhood she had done this in three stages: first throwing the bed-clothes aside and lying until the cooler air imposed the next move; then coming to a sitting position on the edge of the bed and resting there some time; finally standing up and walking. She walked to the full-length oval mirror in its gilt frame, slipped off her nightie and stood for some time appraising herself. She pouted into the mirror and thrust her arms forward, close to her sides, taking the usual satisfaction in her large and exceptionally well-formed breasts. They showed no tendency as yet to sag. She was a tall, solid-boned woman, with substantial shoulders, and the thickness in her upper arms and at the tops of her thighs was firm and rounded. She had a deep complacency about the abundance of her figure which the current quest for fashionable slimness did nothing to dispel. The eyes that looked back at her, in a face still puffy from sleep, were short-lashed, blue and guileless. My fortieth birthday, she thought, and her eyes looked wonderingly at her.

Beginning to feel slightly chilly, she left the mirror and went over to the door where her negligee was hanging. This was of fluffed nylon and the same colour as her nightie – pale mauve was one of her very favourite colours. She opened the door and slipped along the passage to the bathroom where all had been left in order by Donald.

Here she followed her customary procedure: first a warm shower to wash away the grosser impurities of the night, then a prolonged and blissful immersion in water much hotter and frothy with jasmine bath salts, her favourite – she had favourites in everything. Today, however, she had first to wrestle with one of the taps, which had been turned off very tightly. It was leaking too, she noticed, quite badly, and she wondered whether Donald knew. Soon, however, she had forgotten all about it, half-sitting, half-lying in the pale-blue bath, sealed and immune in the hot, scented water, listening to a record-request programme on her transistor radio, Mario Lanza singing 'Santa Lucia'. She lay still, keeping her face carefully out of the water, listening to the powerful voice. Dead now, of course. Sobs built up in the singer's throat in spasm after spasm, and Lavinia felt a languorous response in every fibre.

Cuthbertson had seen the leaking tap immediately after emerging from his shower, and had been distressed by it. The water was escaping steadily, not merely dripping from the mouth of the tap, but welling out at the join higher up, as from a sluggish fountain. He tried tightening it but that seemed to make no difference. The washer perhaps. Or some more fundamental flaw. In any case it would most certainly have to be attended to. Gazing fixedly at the delinquent tap, he resolved on immediate application to the Water Company. He was only restrained from telephoning at once by the thought that the Company's offices would not yet be open. He had a particular hatred for dripping taps, and all leaks, seepages, unauthorized oozings, spilling out from confinement or control.

He mentioned the tap to Mrs Garwood, his housekeeper, while he was eating the breakfast she had prepared, in the little room adjoining the kitchen, where he and Lavinia had their meals when they were not entertaining. His newspaper showed a picture on the front page of widespread destruction and mangled corpses on a city street. A bomb had been planted and detonated at a time of maximum congestion. Such pictures had become commonplace and, occupied as he was with the offending tap, Cuthbertson did not ascertain what city it was, nor which band of enthusiasts was repsonsible. Mrs Garwood told him that the Water Board was repairing faulty taps free of charge in order to prevent wastage. There was a water shortage, apparently.

'A water shortage?' Cuthbertson said, seeing an opportunity to make a joke. 'After all the rain we've been having?'

Mrs Garwood, a grim-faced lady, merely nodded.

At nine o'clock Cuthbertson mounted to his office on the first floor and the first thing he did was to ring the Water Board and report a leakage. The official to whom he spoke promised to send a representative that afternoon.

This settled, he turned his attention to the day's programme. He felt better now, more or less at peace, sitting there at his desk, memo-pad before him, freshly sharpened pencil between his fingers. His early-morning fears, the fiasco with Lavinia, that strange business with the locket, all these things belonged to the messy domestic area; they could not intrude here.

The dark, polished surface of his desk lay before him, empty of clutter, the familiar items in their familiar places: square before him his blotter, edged with dark green leather; to left and right his wire-mesh trays; occupying pride of place dead centre was his pen-rest in chrome and black perspex; and to the right of this, exactly midway between the pen-rest and the edge of his desk, were first his silver cigarette box and then his chunky glass

29

ashtray, forming a little group suggestive of pleasure . . .
Cuthbertson smoked five cigarettes in the course of a working
day, neither more nor less, and at fixed times. The first was due to
be consumed in one hour and twenty-one minutes, at ten-thirty,
with the morning coffee. The deliberate self-control and self-
conquest involved in all this was part of his vision of the School as
a well-ordered society with himself both on its periphery and at its
heart, gatekeeper, ultimate authority, living example. So long as
he shouldered these burdens, kept up these observances, no harm
could come from within or without. Over the years the School had
become associated, in a peculiarly intimate way, with the exercise
of his will; had come to seem dependent on, even hallowed by, a
great number of small self-imposed restrictions, irksome perhaps,
but necessary for him to endure – a sort of personal protocol,
which others might observe, but never fathom.

Something, however, began to trouble him slightly as he
surveyed his desk, a sort of threatening fluidity in the appearance
of things. He moved his large, blunt-fingered hands experiment-
ally, up a little, then down. It was the effect of the light, he
decided. Strange that he had not consciously registered this
before, these vagaries of light across the surface of his desk,
tremulous pools that the movements of his hands minutely
modified. The chrome and perspex melted, froze again. The
numerous facets of the ashtray gleamed in a complex pattern of
intensities. The cigarette box was adrift in its own soft puddle.
Like pools in some road or track of the past after rain, which
change shape and colour as you walk towards them . . . In that
room, above the bay, shapes were constant. The sea light, though
benign, not bleak at all, had seemed shadowless; nothing in that
room ever varied, except their two bodies in relation to each
other. The bay an aimer of white shadowless sea light. Moving,
the movements we made, seemed meaningful, not fully our own
meaning like those of actors, moving in uniform light. I saw her
eyes fill with tears. Before, it was before I actually gave her the
flowers. Did she cry then because she saw something I didn't see? I
was trying to remove the string, twine. Stems that the slightest
pressure of a finger-nail could wound . . .

Cuthbertson braced himself in his seat. There was no time for all that now. He had a number of important things to get straight in his mind. There was a man named Baker, a prospective student, to be seen; there was the interview with Mafferty, due in – he glanced at the clock on the wall – ninety-seven minutes precisely; there were books to be ordered for the literature course; there was the staff meeting, the 'briefing' as Cuthbertson and his second-in-command, Bishop, called it. Following upon all these, and dwarfing them in importance, was the main event of the day, one of the highlights of the term: the Presentation Ceremony. Today was Degree Day. Even then he would not be finished, because there was a Turkish Delegation due in the late afternoon.

All these matters required close attention, and Cuthbertson, a faint glow from his cold shower still persisting, addressed himself to them, in the peace and solitude of his office, with immense determination. But things began to get out of hand almost at once. In spite of all efforts, he could not keep his programme in focus. Events started sliding about. He battled on, mouth dry and chest constricted, not trying now to fix things in sequence, but to shift the creature in the depths of his mind, where it lurked, muddying his thoughts, clouding all attempts at order and logic. Horror grew in him at this monster, and at his own mind, the host, the pasture.

After sitting at his desk in this travail for twenty-three minutes, Cuthbertson had a dreadful headache. He rang for Bishop, Senior Tutor and Administrative Officer, who had a smaller office adjoining. Bishop always did him good.

When Bishop arrived, however, great as was Cuthbertson's need of him, the customary procedure had to be followed. Cuthbertson therefore lowered his aching head to the memo-pad before him and devoted some moments of glazed scrutiny to the words inscribed there. Then he looked up, frowning slightly, his dark luxuriant eyebrows meeting in a line.

'Ah, there you are,' he said, indicating a seat.

Mr Bishop was a balding, big, uneasy man with gentle, considerate manners and a habit of sudden loud laughter. He was not very well qualified academically, as Cuthbertson had always conceded – indeed he had no academic qualifications at all, other than the honorary ones the School had bestowed upon him, but he had been to what Cuthbertson always thought of as One of our Great Public Schools, and this had developed in him valuable qualities of character: a spirit of service, a sense of fair play, and an unswerving loyalty to the leader, all of which qualities were now at Cuthbertson's disposal. He also had a fund of Latin maxims which he was sometimes able to deploy with effect. But it was above all his loyalty, the through-thick-and-thin spirit, which had earned him the position of Administrative Officer, for which he was otherwise not very well-suited, being in a more or less permanent muddle about the detailed running of the School – he relied very heavily on Miss Naylor, the secretary, though he tried to keep this as far as possible concealed from Cuthbertson.

'Not interrupting anything, am I?' Cuthbertson always adopted a brusque commanding-officer style of address with Bishop; it was what he seemed to respond best to. This morning, Cuthbertson noted with approval, the Senior Tutor was dressed in a navy-blue blazer, tan slacks and suede ankle boots. He looked neat and efficient, completely on the ball, somewhat nautical. Cuthbertson felt his headache lifting just at the sight of him. 'Everything in order?' he said.

'Absolutely,' Bishop said. In his tenure of office he had become quite accustomed to this sort of generally phrased, reassurance-seeking question from the Chief. He always answered in a brisk affirmative, whatever his own private confusions. The one thing never to do was to imply doubt or weakness; nothing irritated the Chief as much as that.

'Good, good,' Cuthbertson said, then paused, momentarily at a loss. The stillness in the room, and Bishop's deferential eagerness as he stood there – he seemed not to have noticed the gesture towards the chair – combined for the moment to seem perplexing. At this moment they both heard from below the distant sound of the handbell, rung by Miss Naylor, to signal the beginning of lessons.

'Ah, the bell,' Cuthbertson said, glancing automatically at the clock.

Bishop was not a very clever man, but he was sensitive, in his large and hapless way, and particularly so in anything to do with the Principal, whom he revered. Seeing the bafflement on his chief's brow, he began to supply various administrative details – taking care, however, to refer to matters already known, already discussed; lately he had found the introduction of new matter liable to worry the Chief quite a lot.

'The students have all been informed,' he said, 'about registration dates. As you requested, Donald.' It still gave him pleasure that he was the only one on first-name terms with the chief. 'They have been posted up,' he said. 'And tutors have been asked to remind their groups.'

Cuthbertson roused himself. He had been allowing the Senior Tutor's well-modulated tones to lull him. He must make a contribution. 'What are the dates?' he asked, leaning forward, speaking in a keen, incisive voice.

This question was completely unexpected and the Senior Tutor was thrown by it. There was a rather lengthy silence, then he said, 'I don't remember off-hand, Donald.' He had broken out into a slight sweat. Quite often before this he had been rebuked for his vagueness in the matter of dates and times. He did not seem able to hold such things in his mind. However, his own confusion and the instinct of self-preservation had combined to help him at such moments: he had found that he could sometimes blur the trail by putting things on to a general basis. This was not a matter of policy or cunning, but of allowing his own private miasma to envelop them both. Lately it had been proving increasingly successful.

Now, seeing a flush of annoyance rise to the Chief's face he began to speak quickly, almost at random. 'No excuse if the blighters don't know by now,' he said. 'Some of these fellows . . . It is a difficulty of communication, really, don't you agree, Donald?'

'I don't get your drift,' Cuthbertson said, looking intently at his Senior Tutor.

Bishop paused, trying to order his thoughts, but the Chief's intent regard made this difficult, and after a moment or two he plunged into speech again. 'I am very interested,' he said, 'always have been as a matter of fact, ever since . . . this question of language as, well, let's call it an instrument, for want of a . . . though tool might do. An adequate tool. And whether, in a way, we aren't barking up the wrong tree. I would be really glad of your views on the subject, Donald. Sometime, when you have a free moment, I would just like to put the idea forward, roll it forward, and see you play with it . . .'

He fell silent, aware that the Chief was regarding him with unabated intensity.

'What idea?' Cuthbertson said. He spoke sternly, not wanting his subordinate to know how completely he was failing to follow this discourse.

Bishop paused again, seeking in his personal fog for some form of words that would clinch matters. 'Which came first?' he said, with a sense of breakthrough. 'It is the old hen-and-egg paradox all over again. In more philosophical terms, of course.'

To his relief he saw the Principal begin to nod mildly.

'Language being your hen,' Cuthbertson said. 'Is that what you're getting at?'

'Or your tool,' Bishop said. 'If you take the other alternative.'

'I should have thought that was your egg.'

'What?'

'Your tool.' Cuthbertson frowned. 'Or is there a third possibility?' he said.

'You are going too deep for me now, Donald,' Bishop said.

Cuthbertson smiled. He did not pursue the topic, however, but reverted to the question of registration, saying, 'Remind 'em again in a week or so. Need reminding, most of 'em.'

'They certainly do.'

'Need a chili up their bottoms, some of 'em, eh?'

'Ha, ha, yes, they need a touch of the spur.' Bishop laughed with explosive loudness. Dealing as they did with aliens, most of whom had a very imperfect knowledge of English, or with the naïve and ignorant among their own countrymen, they had developed over the years a joking, belittling habit of speech, the language of dedicated administrators set amidst natives.

'And remember,' Cuthbertson said, when the other's laughter had subsided, 'that fees must accompany applications. I have always regarded that as an axiom. To me, the truly promising student is the one who has paid his fees.'

'Quite so.' Bishop nodded seriously.

'It makes business sense, and it makes academic sense.' Cuthbertson said. 'They concentrate better when they have paid.'

Bishop nodded again, in full sympathy and understanding, and Cuthbertson, taking in once more the other's neat turnout and deferential manner, felt almost if not quite restored.

'All members of staff know about the briefing today, I take it.'

'They have been informed, Donald, yes.'

'There is also the question of Mafferty.' Cuthbertson raised a slow hand to adjust his glasses, which had slipped down his nose a little. 'I had my doubts when I offered him a post here,' he said. 'Unreliable. No sense of responsibility. That was the judgement I formed at the time. But of course we needed someone. And he does have a Cambridge degree. You have checked up on that, I suppose?'

'Er, yes, Donald.' Bishop took out a handkerchief and went through the motions of blowing his nose. The matter of Mafferty's qualifications had been overlooked until quite recently. Miss Naylor had reminded him. They were still waiting for a reply from the university.

'Had it not been for his being a Cambridge man,' Cuthbertson said, 'I should not have employed him in the first place. But it now seems that being a Cambridge man is not, in itself, enough. It has to be backed up by character, and that seems to be missing, in Mafferty's case. Dishevelled. Unpunctual. Smelling of drink. That is the count against him, is it not?'

'Not merely smelling of it, Donald. Actually at times under the influence of. That Persian, I suppose we should call them Iranians now, Taba, his name is, he sometimes passes on bits of information to me, and he told me that he was practically incoherent in the literary appreciation class last week.'

'Taba, eh?'

'Yes, Taba told me that Mafferty — '

'Which group is he in?'

'Who?'

'This Taba chap.'

Bishop scratched breifly at his sparse, sand-coloured hair. 'I'm afraid I don't remember off-hand, Donald.'

'You don't know which group he's in? Good God, man!'

'Well,' Bishop said hastily, 'he was in one group you know, and then he was transferred to another, and so he is still associated in my mind with that group.'

'Which?'

'The one he was in before.'

'Yes, but which one was – '

'He was unsuitable,' Bishop said. He had broken out into a slight sweat again. 'We put these people into groups,' he said. 'It is a great responsibility, don't you think so, Donald? That is another idea I'd like to see you play around with one day. I'd like to roll it down to you, and see you toy with it.'

'What idea?'

'How many degrees of remoteness before it becomes acceptable?'

'That varies,' Cuthbertson said, bluffing. The frequency with which he these days failed to understand his Senior Tutor was one of his numerous worries. 'It varies from person to person,' he said. 'I've always been a great believer in it, myself.'

'Have you?' Bishop too had rather lost the thread. 'You might press the button,' he said. 'But would you use the knife?'

'That is the great question,' Cuthbertson said. 'Did he actually use that word himself?'

'Who, Mafferty?'

'No, Taba. Did he use the word "incoherent" himself?'

'Good Lord, no.' Bishop guffawed. 'You know what their English is like, some of 'em. No, that was his gist.'

Cuthbertson brooded a moment. 'Would you say he was going downhill?' he said.

'Taba?'

'No, Mafferty.'

Bishop pursed his lips. 'I should say he is deteriorating, yes,' he said.

'Going to pieces,' Cuthbertson said. 'Well, I shall be seeing him in the course of the morning. Anything to report on your side, by the way?'

'I shall have to give this fellow Said a talking to. He had been harassing the typing class, passing notes to the girls, couched in language more than affectionate, apparently, and offering costly gifts. Miss Tynsely intercepted one of them, which she describes as obscene. I haven't read it myself.'

Miss Tynsely rented a room on the top floor, in which she taught secretarial skills to small classes of girls. She wore high-necked dresses and brushed her hair right off her forehead.

'Well, keep me posted, won't you? I shall be seeing Mafferty this morning. I shall be ready for him, whatever line he takes.'

'*Praemonitus, praemunitus*,' Bishop said, and he returned smiling to his own office, pleased on the whole with the way the interview had gone. There had been one or two sticky moments, when he had thought he was in for a dressing-down, but he had managed, he thought, to interest the chief in wider issues, just at the right moment.

When the door had closed behind the Administrative Officer, Cuthbertson sat for some minutes in a relaxed position. Then he took a key from a small drawer in front of him, and used it to unlock another drawer, low down on his right. From this he took a folder, dark red in colour, unmarked on the outside. Slipping a hand into the inside pocket of his jacket, he produced a thick black fountain pen. Then, unhurriedly, and with a sense of mastery, he turned to a fresh page and wrote along the top, 'Thought for the Day.' Below this, with barely a moment's pause, he wrote:

Team Spirit, pulling together in a common cause, is of first importance in any enterprise involving collective effort, i.e. human beings working together to one end.

He left a space of one line, then wrote:

Question: How can this spirit be actively fostered?

Answer: The Principal, by unremitting attention to detail, can promote the correct attitudes. i.e. Principal leaves no stone unturned.

He paused for a moment, pen poised. No more words came to him, though it was obvious that the Thought would have to be rounded off. In the stress of composition, he glanced down at the still-open drawer from which he had taken the folder. With a sickening shock of surprise he saw the little gold locket which he had bought for Lavinia lying there. It must have been under the folder. Some of the panic he had felt on not finding it in his

37

dressing-gown pocket returned to him now. Could the mere intention of putting it in his pocket have grown confused with the action itself? Or could putting it in one receptacle, i.e. the drawer, have done service for putting it in another? But in that case . . . My God, he thought, where is certitude to be found? The thing gleamed up at him palely. Hastily he closed the drawer on it.

Into his mind, like a saving vision, sprang the memory of his Senior Tutor's smart turnout that morning.

'An important aspect of this corporate identity is dress,' he wrote eagerly; 'i.e. a decent uniformity is goal.'

His fear was forgotten. The pen between his fingers had become an instrument of power, its ink the irrevocable streaming of his authority. At top speed he wrote:

Teachers must be encouraged by all means to hand to adopt a uniform style of clothing suggested clothing for teachers white shirt plain dark blue tie navy blue blazer fawn slacks chukka or desert boots in dark brown suede.

3

Lavinia's mood of romantic languor, induced by the hot bath and Mario Lanza, was routed completely by the appalling nature of the nine-o'clock news. In tones of polite exuberance, the announcer spoke of economic crisis at home and famine abroad, strikes and the threat of strikes, bomb outrages in various cities, moves to arm the police against rioters. A pitched battle had taken place at Guildford Station between irate commuters and station staff in which two West Indian porters, a ticket clerk, and two members of the public had been injured. A retired colonel, opening a letter, had had his hand blown off. A woman of seventy-eight had been knocked over and trampled upon in a scramble for baked beans at a supermarket. The Prime Minister had been pelted with tomatoes by students in Aberdeen, where he had gone to receive an honorary degree. One had struck him in the face and made it impossible for him to go on with his speech. He was to make a statement, later today – not about that, but about the economic crisis.

Oppressed, Lavinia switched off the set, wishing very much that she had done so earlier. She tried to think of pleasant things, gladioli, pearl earrings, summer dresses. Always, when she was made aware of threats to peace and order, her instinct was to retreat into some safe place, find something nice to think about. This took her usually to what was now inviolable – the past, her childhood. She felt the same alarm now as she had when a girl, when anything threatened to invade her own warm, self-regarding world. The world outside, public events, these were as unreal to her now as they had been then, abstract and meaningless except when they assumed this looming, threatening character. She had no concept of the life of society. Life was a certain acreage, time passing. Life was what she had, at forty.

She soothed herself to some extent with various unguents, talcs, and scents. Then, dressed in a dark-red woollen dress, she went down for her bacon and eggs.

After breakfast, however, she changed her mind about the woollen dress, and changed into a cotton one with little pink flowers on it, because it was turning out such a warm morning. They had got to the middle of May without much warm weather at all, but today it was quite summery. With a white cardigan over her shoulders and a large-brimmed hat with a band of pink ribbon, she set off for town. It was only half a mile or so to the Home, so she decided to walk, and after a few minutes found that she was enjoying it. The warmth of the day, her own gentle motion, lulled her; she relapsed into certain favoured thoughts. She walked in the centre of the pavement, with a sort of deliberate grace, setting one foot very nearly exactly in front of the other. Her head was slightly lowered beneath the wide brim of her hat and her eyes in this partial concealment were hooded and dreaming, not noticing really the laburnum and lilac and mock-orange leaning over the garden fences. Their scents, and the trickling songs of birds in the gardens, not consciously registered, quickened her mood of pleasurable nostalgia.

She was thinking in this dreaming way, musings flecked with sunlight, of freckled, long-lashed Walter, who had once been their gardener, until he had gone away to join the army; the milky skin below the vee of his open-necked shirt; the slightly rougher, slightly redder line of his collar bone; the insolent vacancy of his regard, which hadn't changed much even when . . . The first time, she always thought of the first time with Walter, up against the back of the garden shed, in the midst of a conversation about lupins – she had gone on talking about lupins as long as possible, in an effort to preserve the illusion that what they were doing was in some way related to gardening. Then there was that other time, that hot Saturday. Sunbathing. I went through the trees in my bikini . . .

Mr Honeyball was different, so thin and shy; the fountain-pen clipped in his top pocket; his narrow, shiny shoes. He was pale-skinned, he had that in common with Walter. She hoped they'd have other things in common too – Walter had been in a more or less permanent state of readiness. Mr Honeyball's occupation was more sedentary, of course . . . The sort of skin that one thinks direct sunlight would harm, almost. What would he come as? He would look good as an officer in the Indian Army, when India was under the British, in one of those scarlet tunics. Not the drab khaki they wore now, so utterly unpleasing to the eye . . .

The High Street was crowded. The warmth of the morning, the first real warmth of the year, had brought people out in lighter colours. She thought she saw Mr Mafferty across the street, looking unusually smart in a grey suit. He did not see her. On his way to the School, she thought. He was going to be late, if he was teaching the first hour. There had been trouble with him lately, she suddenly recalled. Donald had made disparaging references. But he was a good-looking man, and very affable in manner. He had a way of looking into your eyes. His own were frequently bloodshot. A drinking man, Donald had said. He was coming to her party too, all the staff had been invited . . . As she drew near the Home, Lavinia began that last-minute resettling of herself which all imminent social occasions required.

Mafferty in fact was not teaching in the earlier part of the morning. He arrived at school some twenty minutes before the mid-morning break, which enabled him to secure the most comfortable chair in the staff-room, have his coffee as strong as he liked it, and make sure of the remaining shortbread biscuits. Even when teaching he was generally able to achieve all these objectives, as he was always out ahead of the others: when the bell went, he stopped at once, often in mid-sentence, and made for the door, defeating by superior footwork any student attempting to waylay him.

Today however, he had a particular sense of leisure and elegance. On this morning of his crucial interview with

Cuthbertson, being dressed more scrupulously than usual, he felt more like a distinguished visitor than one of the teachers. Brushing biscuit crumbs from his best grey suiting, an inch or two of white cuff showing, hair long but scholarly, he hoped to dispel whatever prejudice had accumulated in Cuthbertson's mind against him.

From where he was sitting he could see a portion of the drive leading up to the house, a section of the nearer privet hedge, trimmed and clipped with an almost swooning perfection and immaculateness, in exactly spaced, shallow waves, the very buds and sproutings of nature, Mafferty thought, obedient to Cuthbertson's fanatical sense of order. Farther along, out of sight, but present to his mind, those same hedges culminated in ball shapes and bird shapes, and then the wrought-iron gates and the austerely printed sign, *Regional School of Further Studies. Principal: D. Cuthbertson Ph.D, D.Litt.*

Bit of a misnomer that, old boyo, he imagined himself saying to Cuthbertson, in a natural, unaffected manner. School for Mugs and Crooks would be nearer the mark, eh, what? Offering Cuthbertson a cigar. They both pay the same fee, that's the main point. Well, maybe my turn is coming sooner than you suspect. Old boyo. He thought again of the evening that was coming, his appointment with Weekes at the Metropole. Weekes might have news. They were going into partnership, starting their own School, as soon as they could find suitable premises. You didn't seriously imagine, Cuthbertson, that I would go on indefinitely, putting money into your pockets? Urbanely lighting his cigar for him . . .

He glanced through the window again at the gravel fore-court raked to an almost baffling evenness of surface, the large stone urns of classical shape round the perimeter, containing fuchsias and geraniums. It was speckless. Like a very well-kept cemetery, he thought. But it was the fee-payers, the acquirers of degrees, who were being hallowed here, not the dead. And what is a fellow like Cuthbertson doing, with all that money he had in the bank, what is he doing, spending his days here, hanging about in business suits, like the manager of a hotel, when he could be up and away to Morocco or somewhere? His employer was a mystery to him. If it was me, he thought, and some day it will be, I'd sell up and be off on my travels.

He was in the midst of this transaction, equable but ruthless, when he heard the bell go, and a minute or two later Binks entered the room, looking harassed, which was his usual expression. They exchanged the grimaces of fellow-sufferers without saying anything. Binks went over to get his coffee. His entrance, however, had broken Mafferty's mood. His thoughts became more mundane and more immediate, distaste for his present situation in space and time combining with an irrepressible uneasiness at the coming interview with Cuthbertson.

To allay this, he took from his brief-case the batch of essays handed in by his English Composition class. The subject they had been given was 'Divorce'. Mafferty took out his red ball-point pen and settled down to correct the first one. With pen poised, he began to read the first paragraph:

The cause is: a man's ristriction in a bad way towards a woman. As it has been to my personal intrepidity, divorce is, and is to be one of the most delusive actions in the political phenomena. There is no sophism to anger me so much rather than putting it henceforward and to clarify my opinion that divorce –

He looked up dazed, from this to see Binks sit down at some distance and begin to look closely at a small pocket-book, in which after a moment he began to make notes. Calculating his hire-purchase commitments, Mafferty thought. Binks was a great customer of manufactured goods. Both he and his strapping, square-faced wife were almost uncontrollably acquisitive of articles of furniture and household goods, and spent a good deal of their time negotiating deferred credit purchases, or contriving to postpone payment. In Binks, who was dry and grudging in manner, with a pedantically deliberate mode of speech, this constant feathering of the nest seemed like a secret vice.

'Listen to this,' Mafferty said. He began to read aloud from the essay:

Acts of prostitution, barrenness, quarrels, and impecunious depressments would be of less importance if a man is firm . . .

43

'What on earth is all that about?' Binks said, forming his words carefully.

'Your guess is as good as mine,' Mafferty said.

At this point Beazely entered, his long sparse hair in prophetic disarray, a distant smile on his face. He had been giving his lesson on British Life and Institutions.

'I have just been telling them that the British people live under a dictatorship,' he said. 'It took them completely by surprise.' He advanced into the room with his curiously ungainly, high-stepping walk, and came to rest midway between Binks and Mafferty. 'They weren't prepared for it,' he said.

Mafferty, infusing his tone with irony, said, 'Our parliament is freely elected. Those gentlemen and others at Westminster are making a balls of things by popular consent, yours and mine.'

'Not mine,' Beazely said. 'I never vote.'

Binks looked up from his pocket-book. 'You never vote?' he said.

'Never,' Beazely said. 'It only encourages them.'

'I regard that as irresponsible,' Binks said. The shabby neatness of his suit, his clean-shaved, underfed face – there was never anything left over for personal adornment or indulgence – seemed to offer witness against Beazely. We live in a Democracy, he seemed to be asserting; only in a Democracy do you find people free to run budget accounts, acquire debts. 'Dictatorship indeed!' he said. 'How do you make that out?'

Beazely smiled. He was a tall, very thin man, ungainly of movement, as if he had more than the usual number of joints in his legs. His smiles had a way of disappearing self-approvingly into the folds at the sides of his mouth.

'As an anarchist,' he began and then stopped, as if listening to something outside.

'Dictatorship!' Binks said, looking incredulously at Mafferty.

Beazely smiled again. 'I mean,' he said, 'decisions affecting us closely and made on our behalf by those in authority without our knowledge and consent. Now in a free society – '

Mafferty, who had heard this before, resumed his reading of the essay before him:

Now let us talk over and in shifting towards some less

provocative principal and to forget man's propensities at the
moment but how to protrude.

'How to protrude,' he said, looking up again. 'How to protrude, that is the great issue of our times.'

'We put them there, didn't we?' Binks said.

'That only means that persons in authority are put there by us.'

'That is what I am saying.' Binks looked triumphantly at Mafferty.

'That is what he is saying,' Mafferty said. 'I say, just listen to this.'

Beazely raised one hand. 'Put there by us, to do things for us,' he said. He turned abruptly, stalked towards an armchair and sat down. Binks watched him with narrowed eyes, clearly puzzled.

'But if we put them there . . .' he said.

'My dear fellow they have to be there before they can be discussed at all. If they were not there we would not be discussing them. Your argument is completely circular.'

Let us have no idea, Mafferty read, *of molesting indignation, and treachery towards a woman but to correct. Of course we have made young girls and women to imrpove in prostitution, and to become wild . . .*

'Good God,' Beazely said. 'Who wrote that?'

'Chap called Said.'

'He's the one who's been propositioning Miss Tynsely's girls.'

'He's got a very flowing style,' Mafferty said.

'Now just a minute,' Binks said. 'Is language a means of communication or is it not? You used the word "dictatorship".'

'I did indeed,' Beazely said. 'Advisedly so.'

'Now hang on a minute,' Binks said, 'let us get our terms right. If language is a means of communication, let us get our terms right.'

Mafferty ceased listening, knowing the discussion would lead eventually to Bink's utter confusion. Beazely was unbeatable in argument, being a past master at putting out verbal smoke screens, behind which he retreated, when pressed, to some narrow, unassailable ledge of logic.

The procession of a marriage is very lovely, as well as the procession of divorce if a man should digest it not to be a divorce but a visit or relaxation.

45

Looking up bemused from this, Mafferty saw Bishop entering with a file under his arm. 'Have you finished your coffee?' he said to Mafferty. 'You have? jolly good. Could I have a word with you in my office?'

'By all means,' Mafferty said. Bishop of course would be wanting to prepare him for his interview with the Principal. He put the pages of the essay together, folded them, and put them into his jacket pocket. Then he rose and followed Bishop along the corridor to his office.

This was much smaller than Cuthbertson's and done out in cream and pale blue, a combination that always seemed incongruously dainty to Mafferty. Bishop himself, fidgety, jovial, given to sudden loud laughter, seemed to fill the room and palpitate as it were to the very walls, so that anyone else there felt curiously redundant.

'Take a pew, old man,' Bishop said. He himself went rapidly round behind the desk and opened one of the drawers. There was a short silence, during which Mafferty observed that there were now several water-colour paintings on the wall behind his desk, people doing things on the banks of canals, or sitting in haycarts. He was trying, in a slow, mesmerised way, to picture Bishop going through the business of acquiring them, when the Senior Tutor said, 'I thought it might help if we put our heads together and had a bit of a chat.'

'By all means,' Mafferty said, summoning his goodwill smile.

'I thought it might clear the air.'

Chats with you, Mafferty thought unkindly, tend to have the opposite effect, or such at least has been my experience in the past. They tend to cloud and . . . what was the word?

'I don't believe in beating about the bush,' Bishop said. 'I like to get things out in the open, out in the light of day.'

Obfuscate.

Bishop picked up a pipe from the desk and put it into his mouth. 'I like to get things clear,' he said, speaking rather indistinctly.

'What was that?'

'I said I like to get things clear. The Principal is rather worried about you, Michael.'

'Worried, is he?' Mafferty stopped smiling and frowned to indicate concern.

46

'I'm speaking off the cuff, of course.' Bishop looked seriously at Mafferty as if he very much wanted this point to go home. 'The Principal and I have not cooked up anything over this. We have thought our way through to it separately.'

Mafferty nodded without speaking and after a moment or two Bishop went on, 'He has been under a great deal of stress lately, you know. Perhaps you don't know him as well as I do, but I can see it in his face, in the way he . . . in a score of small ways.'

For the umpteenth time Mafferty wondered whether Bishop had a penchant for Cuthbertson, whether it was some kind of ghastly, emotional involvement that kept him so devoted to the Principal's interests. Bishop was a man who might harbour all manner of lusts and leanings, preserved intact from schooldays in the murk and confusion of his being as in some chemical fluid . . . Dedicated himself to the principle of self-interest, Mafferty found it very difficult to understand any form of altruism, and so he sought, very naturally, by a process of belittlement to bring it within his range. His general method was the attribution of unworthy motives, or stupidity, to any person he had dealings with. Knave or fool was the only decision he had to make about them. He was pretty sure which it was in Bishop's case, but thought he might be kinky too.

'He doesn't want to seem remote and . . . er . . .' Bishop paused, seeking the *mot juste*.

'Inaccessible?' Mafferty suggested.

'Inaccessible, precisely. He wants to be one of us. One of the team. It is an Arthurian idea, basically.'

'Arthurian?' Mafferty said, with a sudden desire to be obstructive. 'I don't believe I've heard of that.' Bishop's moralizing, and that deep-throated, socially irreproachable accent of his, always aroused his hostility in the end.

'Arthurian, did you say?' he said, simulating honest puzzlement.

'You know, the Knights of the Round Table, the King sitting with them . . . *Ex pluribus unus*. No, hang on a tick, that's not it . . .'

'I don't believe I've heard of that,' Mafferty said again, pursing his lips and frowning, as if seeking to perceive a meaning. The

47

man didn't know his arse from his elbow, that was the top and bottom of it. He wouldn't know what he wanted till it was served up to him on a plate. And how often, Mafferty enquired of himself, clear-sighted and wise, how often are the objects of our desire and deepest yearning dished up that fashion? A man has to go forth into the highways and byways, sniff it out like a hound, follow it up. Bishop had a clogged nose, only the hound's loyalty left . . .

'*Primus inter pares*,' Bishop said. 'You know the old tag?'

'No, I don't know her,' Mafferty said. 'Who is it you mean?'

'What?' Bishop removed his pipe.

'Miss who, did you say?'

'I thought since you are a Cambridge man . . .' Bishop said, uncertainly.

'Is she from Cambridge? Do you mean Miss Tynsely? I know her of course.'

'Miss Tynsely?'

'I only say that because I heard you mentioning earlier that you had to interview a student who had been writing love-letters to one of Miss Tynsely's girls, not that I think that is such a grave misdemeanour – '

'They were not love-letters in any accepted sense of the term. They contained lewd suggestions. And it wasn't just one girl, but several.'

'Well, I've just been reading an essay of his, and if that is anything to go on they would have had to concentrate hard to detect lewdness, or anything else. I thought, you see, that you thought that she was making too much fuss of the whole thing, and that was why you referred to her in that disrespectful way.'

'I did not refer to her in a disrespectful way.' Bishop was looking flushed. 'I did not refer to her at all,' he said.

'I'm sorry,' Mafferty said. 'I thought you did. If you'll forgive me saying so, when you speak with the pipe in your mouth, some of your words are indistinct.'

'Now I am going to be absolutely frank with you,' Bishop said, removing his pipe. 'Lateness on the part of the staff cannot be tolerated. And students have complained that you smell of drink.'

'They smell of worse things, some of them,' Mafferty said. He was indignant.

'I daresay they do, old man,' Bishop said. 'Now, if he raises any of these points, just accept them without demur, will you? Because, not to mince matters — and if there's one thing I dislike more than another it's a fellow who goes beating about the bush, bring it out in the open, give it an airing, that has always been my practice — '

Probably what you do in the park on Sundays, Mafferty thought. Flasher written all over you. 'It's a good principle,' he said. 'Excellent.'

'Well,' Bishop said, 'to be absolutely frank with you, it is your general attitude that is at fault. Now I am not saying that I see it his way entirely, but he's very shrewd in his judgements, you know, very shrewd; we've got to remember that he built this business up from scratch, the place was falling to pieces, so I'm told, but he saw the possibilities right from the start. *Venit, vidit, vicit.*'

'Excuse me, I don't quite — '

'Like the great Julius, you know.'

Seeing the expression of puzzlement return to Mafferty's face, Bishop said hastily, 'The point is that he has very definite ideas about the way things should be done here, and he needs careful handling, especially today, he's very tense today, today is Degree Day, as I hardly need to remind you . . .'

'You mean I should humour him,' Mafferty said, but realized at once that he had gone too far.

'Now just hold on a tick,' Bishop said, regarding him with an unusual and rather disturbing directness. 'I don't like that kind of remark.'

Mafferty became disagreeably aware of the primitive bulk of the man behind the desk. If Bishop were ever able to see anything clearly enough to act on it he would be formidable.

'If you don't show the right attitude,' Bishop said, 'you'll probably get your marching orders on the spot. No one is indispensable, you know.'

Mafferty kept his sense of outrage well away from his face. 'Right,' he said. 'Thank you for telling me. I won't forget it.' Won't forget either of you, he thought. Creeps. Well, my turn is coming. Maybe sooner than you think, old boyo. Maybe sooner than you bloody well think. It depended on Weekes really.

'I regard it as a real favour, you taking me aside in this way,' he said.

Bishop was still regarding him rather closely, '*Praemonitus praemunitus*', he said. 'There's a lot of truth in it.'

At the Royal Albert Hall last night, said Mrs Greenepad's radio, *where five thousand company chiefs were attending the Institute of Director's annual conference –*

Her room-mate, Mrs Mercer, had slipped down the passage for a word with Mrs Oakley, and Mrs Greenepad had taken vindictive advantage of this to switch on, just catching the ten-thirty news summary.

The former Coal Board chairman referred to strikes as the 'Achilles heel' of our society and attacked . . .

I'll teach her, Mrs Greenepad thought, to contradict her betters about the echelons of the B.B.C. Making up her face and looking at workmen. Putting the margarine out. Fury at the recollection of all this insulting behaviour made Mrs Greenepad grind her dentures. Sitting there on her fanny listening to news items on a radio not her own . . .

Two more of the victims of the bomb outrages which took place late yesterday evening have died in hospital, bringing the total of deaths to twenty-five. It is still not clear which terrorist group was responsible.

In Bangladesh attempts at famine relief are reported to have come too late to save the inhabitants of the worst affected areas. Here is Barrington Smallbeam, our correspondent in Dakkar: What remains of Sabed Ali's family is still together, squatting on the concrete floor of the gruel kitchen outside Rangpur. He told me their younger daughter died yesterday, and his wife Sultana nodded with no sign of –

At this moment Mrs Mercer came back into the room, and Mrs Greenepad switched her radio off. However, Mrs Mercer was so eager to impart news she had just heard from Mrs Oakley that she affected not to notice this.

'You know Mrs Wass?' she said.

'Of course I know Mrs Wass.'

'Well she was standing outside Tesco's yesterday afternoon

when they started selling some baked beans they had just got in, and when the people outside heard about it they all started rushing to get in the queue and Mrs Wass got knocked down in the rush and she broke her hip.'

'Asking me if I know Jenny Wass.'

'She's in hospital now and Mrs Oakley says she's on the critical list.'

'I knew her before you ever came here.'

'They was like wild animals, Mrs Oakley says.'

'Well, if people will stand outside stores during a baked beans crisis, they must abide by the consequences.'

'Considering you have known her such a long time,' Mrs Mercer said, with sudden spirit, 'you don't seem – '

At this moment there was a knock at the door.

'That will be my visitor,' Mrs Mercer said. She looked hard at her room-mate, but Mrs Greenepad made neither movement nor sound.

Lavinia knew that something was wrong, the minute she entered the room. Normally, by a tacit arrangement, when one or the other of the old ladies had a special visitor, the other vacated the room until the visit was over. On this occasion, however, Mrs Greenepad made no move to leave. Indeed, she seemed to settle herself more firmly in the armchair in her half of the room – the room was divided exactly between them, and every inch was accounted for. It was obvious in any case, even without that basilisk immobility, that Mrs Greenepad had decided to include herself in the visit, because she had taken pains with her appearance. Her scanty white hair had been wetted and combed carefully and she had a new-looking, pale-blue woollen jacket on. Her little, red-rimmed eyes surveyed Lavinia with an expression at once derisory and composed.

'Oh, good-morning, Mrs Greenepad,' Lavinia said brightly. 'How nice to see you.'

'Good-morning.' Mrs Greenepad made no effort to respond to the question implicit in these last words.

'How are you this morning, Mrs Mercer?' Lavinia said, turning her look of determined brightness that way.

'It is kind of you to enquire.' Mrs Mercer never answered

queries as to her health or feelings directly, allowing them to emerge or be distilled from the general tenor of her speech. 'Very kind of you, as I always say, and I appreciate it, finding time to visit a lonely old woman. No one could call *me* lacking in appreciation, not like some, that has friends for twenty years and then can't take no interest when they get trampled on, and their hips broken.'

'Dear me,' Lavinia said. 'Who trampled on her?'

'She got caught in a baked beans rush.'

'Dear me,' Lavinia said again. 'Look, I've brought you some apricots, the first of the year.' She took a brown paper bag from her shopping basket, and laid it on Mrs Mercer's little table.

'Forced, I shouldn't wonder,' Mrs Greenepad said, spitting inadvertently.

'Yes,' Mrs Mercer said. 'Thank you, dear, but there are people in this world without the milk of human kindness anywhere about them, not like you.'

She shifted her large body indignantly in the armchair, and raised mottled hands to her hair, which in spite of more determined efforts than usual she had not succeeded in ordering. This mass of brown hair, from which outsize hairpins were constantly detaching themselves, hanging off or actually falling, had always seemed to Lavinia intimately connected with the old lady's style of speech, which was a constant struggle to prevent the escape of noises that were not words.

'My son and daughter-in-law came on Saturday,' Mrs Mercer said, feeling in her hair. She said no more for the moment, merely sat, emitting the tiny, incessant sounds that had lately become characteristic of her. During the past few months she had developed a sort of sucking, savouring habit of the mouth, as if she had some tiny sweet in there, permanently central.

'How are they getting on?'

'Some people come to see you,' Mrs Mercer said, 'but more out of a sense of duty. I don't mean you, dear. *They* only come once a month.'

Mrs Greenepad coughed with surprising loudness, and tapped both heels on the floor.

'Dear me,' Lavinia said. 'We *are* in the doldrums today, aren't we? Your son and daughter-in-law live in Sheffield, remember *that*, Mrs Mercer. That is a long way from here. It is really very good of them to come and see you so regularly. They have small children, too. I remember you telling me.'

'Three,' Mrs Greenepad said suddenly, in her dry, snapping voice. 'And they are so above themselves, you would not credit it.'

An ominous silence descended on the room. Lavinia looked for some moments at the hall above Mrs Greenepad's neat bed. It was decorated with embroideries, the work of Mrs Greenepad herself, who had retrained in old age her nimbleness with the needle. One in particular stood out, a garden crowded with flowers of every hue. Beneath in stitched copperplate, were the words, 'Let's gather Flowers, instead of Thorns, the World is what We make it.'

It was while she was puzzling over the meaning of those words, in particular what was meant by gathering thorns, that Mrs Mercer said, 'I'll walk along the passage with you,' just as if Lavinia had suggested leaving.

Outside the door, in whispers, the story of the quarrel came out. Some disagreement arising from a news bulletin, Lavinia gathered, though she couldn't quite make out the details.

'That's not the real reason,' Mrs Mercer said. 'Her nephew that used to come every week has gone to Canada. She had a friend that sometimes came, but she died. She never has visitors now. That is why she's taken against me. She'd never admit it, though. Now she won't let me listen to her table radio. When I come in she switches it off.'

'Why don't you ask for a new room-mate?'

'Put in for a transfer? There's a waiting list as long as your arm. Every person in this Home wants a transfer. You have to wait months for a change, and inside a week you are not on speaking terms. It isn't worth it.'

'And she won't let you listen to her radio at all?'

'She switches it off when I come in. She waits till I'm inside, then switches off.'

Lavinia had had a charitable impulse, but she said nothing about this to Mrs Mercer. She merely reminded the old lady about her party that evening.

'The taxi will come for you at nine-thirty,' she said.

'I'll be ready for him,' Edwina said. She craned her head forward suddenly. 'Listen,' she said. The sound of a male voice was coming from the room behind them. 'She's got it on again,' Edwina said, looking intently at Lavinia.

'Don't worry,' Lavinia said. 'Everything is going to be all right.'

She left shortly after this and made her way back along the High Street. Here, in an electrical goods emporium, she inspected several radios, choosing finally a large portable set, which she paid for by cheque and arranged to have delivered to Mrs Mercer at the Home.

While she was making her way to the taxi-rank, she saw a mad person. He was short and fat and joyously smiling. He stopped frequently in his walk, raising his round unshaven face to the sky, and making a gesture with arms extended, palms upward, as if in blessing.

4

The first of several checks and frustrations experienced by Baines on this day was caused by the fact that there was no theatrical costumier in the town. He had to apply to the local repertory theatre, where, after a good deal of discussion, they agreed to let him hire a costume. There were no masks, but he was able to obtain dark glasses and a false moustache.

He returned to his room with a costume, left it there, and retrieved the brown carrier bag from its hiding place under his bed. When he left again he was carrying this. He was early for his appointment and since it was a warm sunny morning he decided to walk. In the High Street he was stopped by a girl rattling a famine-relief tin. She stuck a little blue flag in his lapel and gave him a pamphlet, with a picture of a naked, starving African woman on the cover. Baines thrust this into his pocket. He was beginning to feel anxious, now that the meeting with the man he knew of as Kirby was imminent.

The meeting-place was in the area of waste ground known locally as The Tips, which lay on the other side of town, beyond the railway station and the canal, a desolate hummocky area of considerable extent, full of hollows, sudden steep declivities and pits, combed with narrow clay paths that led nowhere except to intersections with other paths, or into tangled slopes of bramble and willowherb. The area owed its name to the fact that years previously many tons of earth and rubble had been dumped here and left. Now the mounds and slopes had settled, softened with vegetation, and the whole area had taken on an identity quite distinct and separate from any other part of the town. It was a refuge for vagrants and drinkers, who made little shelters for themselves in the remoter hollows, and a place of resort for all those who had no work to do, and for alienated or outcast people.

It was to this place, the ridge that ran along the upper part of it, where the clay was covered with rank glass, that Baines made his way, carrying his little brown bag, whistling between his teeth. Here the man named Kirby should be waiting for him just below the ridge where it levelled, where one could stand against the bankside, more or less screened from view. He did not know Kirby by sight but he would be wearing a white flower in his buttonhole – sufficiently unusual, it had been thought at Headquarters, to provide identification, given the coincidence of time and place. On a level area just before the ridge began, a thin, red-haired man was standing on a box addressing a small knot of listeners. 'Oh my dear friends,' Baines heard him say, 'Jesus died on the cross for you.'

Baines went past with averted face. After some minutes he saw from above a man sitting against the bankside below the ridge. He made his way down the narrow path towards this person. When he drew near, the man turned his head and Baines found himself regarding a youngish, plump man with a white face and a soft-looking, unpleasantly vivid mouth. Some limp daises looked out of the top pocket of his stained and shabby blue suit. Could this be regarded as a button-hole? Baines wondered. He stood there for some moments in something of a quandary. Then he decided to try the first line of dialogue that had been pre-arranged up at Headquarters.

'It is a good day today,' he said.

The other man smiled a gap-toothed smile and began fumbling in the pockets of his jacket. After a moment he took out a piece of paper which Baines recognized as one of the pamphlets the girl in the High Street had been handing out.

'Looka them tits,' the man said, holding out the paper invitingly towards Baines. 'Looka them tits.'

After a moment Baines realized that he was referring to the drooping breasts of the emaciated African woman on the front of the pamphlet. This could not be Kirby.

'Clear off,' Baines said, in a voice thick with loathing. 'Get away from here.' He took a step towards the other man, raising a fist.

The man got up quickly, went at a rapid shambling walk diagonally away up the hillside. This obedient promptness made it seem as if he had expected to be ordered away. Baines found himself trembling slightly: he had always felt a horrified repugnance for sick or abnormal people; he was daunted too by the coincidence of finding someone in just this place, wearing what might have been taken as a buttonhole. He was still staring up the hillside, though the man had disappeared now, when he heard a voice behind him, saying, 'It is a good day.'

Baines turned, and found himself facing a man of about his own age, short and thickset, with a white carnation in his buttonhole. 'I'm supposed to say that,' he said. 'Not you.'

'Better ones coming,' the other man said promptly. He had very pale, quick-glancing eyes.

'Better for all of us,' Baines said. He held out his hand and the other man shook it. 'You should have waited for me to speak,' Baines said. 'Here it is.' He handed over the brown bag. 'It is set for eleven-fifteen tonight,' he said. 'You can plant it whenever you like. All you have to do is press – '

'I know what to do.'

'You have had your instructions, I suppose,' Baines said. 'Do you know the town well?'

'Well enough. I know where the Municipal Art Gallery is. That is all I need to know.'

'Municipal Art Gallery? But it is the Conservative Committee Rooms you are supposed to blow up.'

'My instructions are to cause maximum damage to the Municipal Art Gallery.'

'I don't understand,' Baines said. 'I made personal representations at Headquarters. This is the first I have heard of the Municipal Gallery as a target. From whom did you get your instructions?'

'I am not at liberty to say.'

'But surely,' Baines said, 'the question should be – '

'Looka them tits,' a soft sibilant voice said behind them.

Turning sharply, Baines saw the white-faced, shambling character whom he had driven off before, now standing only a few feet away from them, holding out the crumpled pamphlet. He had approached quietly, over the grass.

'Looka them tits,' he said again, not venturing closer, but leaning forward, holding out the picture of the dying African woman, his soft, too-red lips curving in a gentle smile.

'You filthy – ' Baines said. He stared at the smiling man, his mouth dry with rage and loathing.

'Shall I stretch him?' Kirby said, with immediate savagery. 'I'll knock your teeth in,' he said. 'You bloody pervert.'

'Don't touch him,' Baines said. 'We don't want to attract attention to ourselves. Get away from here,' he said to the man, taking a step forward.

With the same curious promptness as before, the man began to back away. He backed for some yards, then turned and made off, at the same rapid, shambling pace.

Baines turned to face Kirby again. He felt shaken by this reappearance. 'We'd better go our separate ways,' he said. He looked closely at the other's face for a moment or two, at the narrow forehead, pale unsteady eyes. Kirby did not look a very intelligent type of man.

'I still don't understand this confusion over the target,' Baines said. 'But you must follow your instructions, I suppose.'

'There were them that wanted the Conservative Committee Rooms,' Kirby said, 'and them that wanted the Municipal Art Gallery. And a third school of thought that felt it didn't make no difference.'

'They know what they are doing, up at Headquarters,' Baines said loyally. 'There are some very shrewd people up there.'

'I daresay we shall manage,' Kirby said, gripping the bag, turning away.

'Odd,' Baines said. 'If it is the Art Gallery, I shall be at a party in the next road.'

'Well, Mr Baker,' Cuthbertson said. 'Perhaps you could give me some indication of your requirements?'

He looked steadily through his glasses at the person seated opposite, across the desk. He liked the sober suiting and deferential posture of this person. The letter before him was illiterate in phrasing. On the basis of the letter he had formed certain prognostications. It was deeply reassuring, when there was so much lately to frighten and confuse him, to find that these had been entirely correct: this was a person who had worked hard, accumulated capital in some lowly calling, and now wished to better himself.

Cuthbertson had realized at a very early stage that all applicants could be divided into two main categories: self-improvers and careerists. The former, naïvely vain and self-deceiving, were able to regard the degrees awarded by the School as both worthless and worth having; the latter had no such illusions, intending to use the degrees in areas of the world where their true nature might be kept indefinitely concealed. This great perception, though the basis of the School's prosperity, Cuthbertson had of late years largely ceased to acknowledge, even to himself, as it conflicted with his sense of the School as a force for good. None the less it was useful on occasions like the present, when a student might slip off the hook if clumsily handled.

'We make it our endeavour,' he said, 'to, ah, tailor the needs of the . . . to, ah, tailor the instruction to the needs of the individual student.'

Gentle brown eyes returned his regard. The man had a weatherbeaten face, thinning hair. He leaned forward, keeping his knees unpresumptuously together. Cuthbertson smiled, aware of the power at his disposal, power as it were diffused through all the appurtenances of his office, particles of power rebounding from the quiet walls and gleaming surfaces; all emanating from himself, the generating and controlling force. An urge rose in him to keep absolutely still, keep this generative power at its optimum, sit there for ever, no fear or doubt admitted, in absolute immobile mastery, dominating Mr Baker throughout eternity. His hands rested heavy on the desk before him. Something, however, some alien element in the room, only vaguely sensed before, now began more definitely to trouble and disturb him. His hands moved, and he glanced momentarily aside.

'You spoke of history in your letter,' he said.

'Yes,' Mr Baker said. 'Yes, I've always been interested in history, right from my school days. That is going back a bit.'

'You will find a number here of your generation,' Cuthbertson said, smiling, moving his hands restlessly on the desk.

'Of course we wasn't well taught,' Mr Baker said.

'Some of the teaching in our schools leaves much to be desired,' Cuthbertson said. 'We often find ourselves having to do a certain amount of remedial work before the true process of education can begin. Which of our history courses are you interested in? You've seen the prospectus, I take it?'

'I'm more interested in the modern, really. It helps you to understand your own society more, doesn't it?'

'That is an interesting point of view,' Cuthbertson said. 'Mr Mafferty does Modern History. A very keen, incisive mind. He is a Cambridge man.'

Thinking of Mafferty caused him to glance at the clock. It was a quarter to eleven. He was again troubled by a returning sense of something different about the room, something not quite right. He glanced around uneasily. Nothing seemed out of place . . .

'I didn't want just a correspondence course, you know,' Mr Baker said.

'Oh, no, no, no.' Cuthbertson bestirred himself, looked back with something of an effort at his prospective student's face. 'The student-teacher relationship is of the essence of our system here, of the absolute essence,' he said.

Mr Baker leaned forward suddenly. Great earnestness marked his demeanour. 'I would like to obtain a degree,' he said.

'That would be the twelve-week course to the first degree, the Bachelor of Arts, or Science.'

'Would that entitle me to put B.A. after my name?'

'Certainly, certainly. And to a certificate which you would be at liberty to frame and display, if you so wished.'

'The terms for that . . .' Mr Baker said.

'For the twelve-week course,' Cuthbertson said, knowing the other knew already, 'the inclusive fee – '

At this point, however, he fell silent, again glancing round the room. Stray peppering thoughts began to bombard him, sensations rather, that he could not isolate or meet squarely. He looked at the immaculate expanse of dark-blue carpeting, the fawn armchairs, the two low tables, the cushioned window seat. Everything was in exact position, as it always was . . .

Mr Baker coughed, and Cuthbertson thought he saw an

expression of embarrassment or uncertainty on the other's face. 'Of the absolute essence,' he said, as if there had been no intermission. 'Or such, at least, is our belief.'

Suddenly, he realized what the matter was: it was scent, not sight, that was being offended. There was a faint alien sweetness in the air, disturbing the usual plushy, neutral odours of his office. Some perfume, perhaps, that Mr Baker . . . He did not look that kind of man. The scent, once recognized, seemed stronger now, it pervaded the room like a leak of something dangerous. Cuthbertson shifted his bulk in the chair and opened his mouth, with a sudden audible intake of breath.

'Are you feeling all right?'

'I beg your pardon?' Cuthbertson blinked several times. Mr Baker's long-jawed weatherbeaten face resettled into focus. 'Excuse me,' Cuthbertson said. 'I have a lot on my mind today. Today is Degree Day, you know. It is also my wife's birthday. And there is a delegation from Turkey coming to be shown round. We were discussing . . .'

'Fees,' Mr Baker said.

'For the twelve-week course,' Cuthbertson said, reverting smoothly to the point at issue, 'the inclusive fee for tuition and degree is seven hundred and fifty pounds. Payable in advance. That is the honours course. The general degree comes to one hundred and fifty less.'

'I think I'd be more interested in the honours.'

'Quite right,' Cuthbertson said. 'One must aim high. You are the sort of student we want here, Mr Baker. There is one condition, however, which is also mentioned in the prospectus.'

'Condition?'

The smell seemed to be getting stronger. A voice at once his own and another's urged Cuthbertson to his feet, to seek out and destroy this subversive sweetness. He sat there some moments longer, looked fixedly at Mr Baker. Then he stood up abruptly, moved out from behind his desk, turned his head this way and that. Aware that this behaviour, however necessary, might seem eccentric to Mr Baker, he went on talking in a manner as equable as possible. 'Yes,' he said, 'the course must be completed satisfactorily on your part. If not, you would be charged for tuition only, part of the fee would be refunded, and the degree would not be awarded.'

'How do you mean, satisfactorily?'

Cuthbertson looked round. Mr Baker had turned in his chair and was watching him alertly.

'I mean as to conduct,' he said beginning to walk slowly forward near to the wall. We cannot permit, the voice said. Oh dear me, no. The voice was bland, remorseless, and often omitted verbs. A certain give and take, yes, but not this. 'Conduct, attendance, that sort of thing,' he said. 'And style of dress. We like to see students wearing ties, for example. Navy blue is a colour we favour. We find that uniformity of appearance encourages the sense of community we are aiming at. Yes.'

Reaching a point about half-way along the wall, Cuthbertson stopped and turned inwards. This enabled him to see that Mr Baker had also risen and was standing with his hands on the back of his chair, watching him intently.

'I thought you meant failing the exam,' Mr Baker said, laughing falsely.

Cuthbertson looked gravely for some moments at this laughing face of Mr Baker. 'There is no examination,' he said. 'The matter rests with the tutor's report.'

After a moment he resumed his soft, circumspect padding, moving this time across the room, towards the opposite wall. Coming to one of his fawn armchairs he edged and felt his way cautiously round it. The scent was strong now, and Cuthbertson was beginning to feel personally endangered, as if a scented pad were being moved slowly and inexorably towards his mouth. He felt it to be vitally necessary to go on talking, to preserve the structure of the interview and keep his own fears at bay. 'Each student,' he said, 'is taught individually, with particular reference to his abilities and general attainment. Progress is necessarily relative, depending as it does on the level of the student at the beginning of the proceedings. Degrees are awarded in accordance with this relative assessment.'

He thought he heard Mr Baker say something somewhere behind him. 'Quite so,' he said, without looking round. He could get no clue as to where the smell might be coming from, and Mr

Baker's presence inhibited him from making a thorough-going search. He raised his face towards the ceiling and sniffed delicately twice. Hearing a movement behind him he turned sharply but Mr Baker was in the same position. More strongly than before he had the sense of a scented, suffocating pad being moved slowly towards him. He opened his mouth to get more air. With an instinct of survival he sought to stopper the scent with some memory, find in the past a container for this muffling pad that threatened to cut off all senses with his breath . . . A certain give and take, yes, the voice said, very clearly and distinctly. But this, this cannot be permitted. Daffodils, the white light. No, daffodils are scentless . . . With a heaving of the mind he had it, just in time, honeysuckle. August honeysuckle, the smell of it in the hedges and on our hands.

'Honeysuckle', Cuthbertson said. He stood in the middle of the room, stilled by the memory. The pad receded. Remembering Mr Baker, he said, 'Relative assessment and capacity credit marking. None of the older foundations have been prepared to adopt it. Hidebound, you know. Of course, as I point out in my . . . in the Prospectus, our degrees are not everywhere recognized, our graduates sometimes meet with prejudice.'

He was moving now along the top end of the room, towards the book case. 'That is settled then,' he said. 'The School Secretary, the invaluable Miss Naylor will give you any further details you require as to . . . I look forward to having you in the student body, on the Modern History Course, Mr Baker, and it only remains for me to say . . . Subject to the payment of fees, of course . . .' Honeysuckle, that was it. Afterwards we lay down on the bankside, still with the honeysuckle, and she said, be careful, take care, you will crush the honeysuckle. She meant something else. What did she mean?

'You will find your fellow students a very cosmopolitan and variegated community,' Cuthbertson said, feeling about among the books, speaking faster and faster. 'We have persons of every sort and condition here, united of course by a common desire for self-improvement and interest in the things of the mind, drawn, they are drawn from all quarters of the compass, your real traditional type of wandering school, you will find every race and creed here and a considerable variety in pigmentation and texture of hair that is part of our purpose part of our philosophy to submerge ah immerse the student in this cultural pool . . . Aha!'

He had seen them, on a narrow cabinet in the recess beyond the bookshelf. Hyacinths they were, not honeysuckle, a little bunch of white and blue hyacinths, in a Wedgwood vase, behind the petroleum company calendar. Odd, secretive place for them to be. They must have been put there sometime during the morning. A word to the secretary would not come amiss. Somehow, though, he did not think it was Miss Naylor's doing . . . He advanced slowly and cautiously on the flowers. 'Former students,' he said, 'we like to feel, who have gone their several ways, still continue to have this sense of having been, so to speak, dipped . . . "Excuse me," one of them might say to another, meeting by chance in some . . . "Excuse me, but isn't that a Regional College of Further Studies tie you are wearing?" '

Reaching forward with a sort of stealth, Cuthbertson seized the flowers and drew them out of the vase. He looked over his shoulder smilingly. 'There is a little counter in the secretary's office,' he said, 'where ties, scarves – '

Suddenly he realized that his office no longer contained Mr Baker. Without word or sound of any kind, Mr Baker had gone. Odd behaviour, Cuthbertson thought. Unmannerly.

Standing there alone, however, in the silence of the room, holding the dripping bunch in his hands, he was unable for long to resist the suspicion that he had somehow mismanaged the interview with Mr Baker. He was aware, with alarm, of having acted under some kind of duress. A certain give and take, yes. Distracting odours, evocations of past faces and events – not in a well-run institution. You will crush the honeysuckle, she said. Her face closer than it had ever been. Her mouth smiled and then stopped smiling. Afterwards. . . .

He was standing thus when a light knock came at the door. Unthinkingly he called, 'Come in.' The door opened and a smarter than usual Mafferty came into the room, smiling sociably. Only then did Cuthbertson remember his appointment with this lax fellow, and become aware at the same time of the strangeness, for somebody else, of finding the Principal, standing in the middle of the room, holding dripping flowers.

'I am just disposing of a few flowers,' he said.

'Good idea,' Mafferty said briskly, determined to agree with everything.

Cuthbertson went back to his desk, tore off a few pages from his memo pad and wrapped the flowers up in a wet ball. This he dropped into the waste paper basket. Taking a large white handkerchief from his top pocket, he made a thorough job of wiping his hands, looking steadily at Mafferty while he did so.

Meanwhile, in the adjoining office, Bishop was in the midst of his interview with Said, the Somali student.

'Now I daresay,' he was saying, 'that in your part of the world they do things differently. I am an old stager; I am quite prepared to admit that standards vary throughout the world, I wouldn't want you to go away thinking that your Senior Tutor is unaware of the relative nature of customs and practices, but when in Rome, you know, you must do as the Romans.'

Said, a handsome, slender negro with a reserved manner and very discoloured whites to his eyes, kept his gaze on the wall before him.

'Is it proverb?' he said.

'Never mind that now. Miss Tynsely has complained. She has turned over to me those notes you wrote to various of the student typists. In this country it just isn't done to write notes of that kind to girls you do not know. It is *infra dig*. I have them here before me, and I must say . . . Take this one for example.'

He picked up a mauve sheet of paper from his desk. Adopting a deliberately dry and unimpassioned tone, he read, ' "And I will deposit you with golds and for the blisses there will be more golds and maybe bracelets of my people." '

There was a short silence during which Said did not acknowledge by any flicker of expression the authorship of these words.

'I mean to say,' Bishop said, 'wrap it up how you will, that definitely amounts to an offer of money for favours received. Here's another one: "At home I am prince and I am used by my religion to contain everything by mind over matter inside me

65

going into traces and so you can have multiple funs – " That is from the note to Miss Barrett,' Bishop said. 'Perhaps you didn't know it, but her father is a militant type of man . . . Apart from anything else, there is the quality of your English. People do not have funs.'

Said glanced quickly towards him. 'They have funs and games,' he said.

'They may have games,' Bishop said, 'but they do not have funs.'

Said took from an inside pocket a small notebook and a pencil. 'Games but not funs,' he said. 'Excuse me.' He wrote something in the notebook. After a moment he looked up with a slight, dignified smile, and said, 'Englishmen are good in games but not in funs, isn't it?'

'Good *at*,' Bishop said. 'No, it isn't. I mean no, they aren't. Anyway they are. Just as good as any one else, that is. You are missing the whole point which is that the word has no plural. Never mind that now. Look what you say in your note to Miss Birdwood.' Picking up yet another sheet, he read, ' "I want to put diamonds exactly in the centre of your both teats very much." '

Bishop laid down the paper and looked sternly at Said. 'Now I am the first to understand an ardent temperament,' he said, 'but that note is definitely suggestive. I mean you are actually offering . . . The word is "nipples", by the way. We don't speak of the centres of teats. It has an odd ring in English. Now the fact that several of the girls have received similar missives – '

'How you spell that?' Said said. 'With two bs, aren't they?' His pencil was poised over the notebook.

'Missives? No, double – '

'No, instead of centres of teats.'

'Double *p*, man. Otherwise it would be "nibbles".' Bishop laughed with sudden explosive loudness. 'That means to take little bites,' he said.

He continued to laugh at this idea for some moments.

Said looked at him with a flickering, distrustful expression, then transferred his gaze to the wall. With a dignified gesture of finality he returned notebook and pencil to his pocket.

'*Ex Africa semper aliquid novi*,' Bishop said, reverting to seriousness. 'Now as I was saying, the fact that several of the girls have been the objects of your attention seems to suggest, to our Western way of thought, that this is not a case of romantic attachment. It is not so much the personality and appearance of some particular girl that has attracted you, but a sort of generalized desire for bodies, Said. There is an unpleasing plurality about it. I haven't actually sounded the girls concerned, but I'm willing to bet my bottom dollar they felt, ah, belittled.'

Said's eyes flickered at the idiom, but he made no move towards his notebook.

'Besides,' Bishop said, 'what is all this about being a prince? I understood you to be a trainee controller at Mogadishu airport. That is false pretences, old boy.'

Bishop paused, regarding the other closely, in an effort to see if his words were having any effect. Said's forehead glistened. His lips were pale lilac in colour. They were full, and set in a slight pout, which gave his mouth the appearance of a crumpled rose.

'Now I consider myself,' Bishop said, 'since you are so far from home, in *loco parentis*, so to speak, and if there is anything at any time that I can do for you, if the pressure gets too great to bear alone, and believe me, I know something of pressures of that kind, we are all human, Said, more so than you might think . . . I am always available here at my office or at home if you prefer it, always ready to lend a sympathetic . . . so if ever you feel like a chat, feel like getting something off your chest, I am always . . . But you must stop soliciting the student typists, otherwise you will be imperilling your degree. You could find yourself returning to Mogadishu without a certificate of any kind, and that might well have a blasting effect on your future career at the airport.'

There was a light knock at the door and Miss Naylor, the secretary, came in with Bishop's share of the second mail. She put it on the desk, smiled at Bishop, gave Said a neutral look, and said, 'What have you been doing to Mr Baker?'

'Who? I don't believe – '

'The new student. He came and asked for his registration fee back. Said he'd changed his mind about the course. I told him that the registration fee is not refunded under any circumstances.'

'The Principal interviewed him, I believe.'

'Probably one of these unbalanced types,' Miss Naylor said. 'There are a lot of them about these days.'

Miss Naylor had a beautiful figure, shown off to good advantage by the tight blouse and short skirt she was wearing. Said watched her progress to the door and the petals of his lips moved, as if he were interiorly phrasing fresh blandishments.

'Well, I hope you will keep it in mind,' Bishop said, without much conviction. His interview with Said had taken longer than he had expected; he had a lesson now, and so it was not for another hour that he was at leisure to look through his mail, and to discover that it included the answer to his queries about Mafferty.

'Now I must tell you, Mr Mafferty,' Cuthbertson said, seating himself behind his desk, 'that there have been, ah, complaints regarding your teaching.'

'Complaints?' Mafferty attempted to infuse the word with mingled disbelief and amused indulgence, but succeeded only in sounding weakly remonstrant.

'As to your time-keeping, and also, not to put too fine a point on it, your sobriety.'

Cuthbertson placed his blunt finger-tips together. This seemed to complete a sort of circuit, for his voice at once took on the steady hum of power. 'Now you are a young fellow,' he said, 'just starting out on your career. The world is your oyster, Mafferty, but let me tell you this, success has to be *earned*. You have to put your shoulder to the wheel right from the very word go. I am thinking of the School, primarily, I won't deny that, of this corporate enterprise we have built up, I like to think together, one for all and all for one, but I am thinking of you too, sitting here today on the threshold. It is not in your interest that unpunctuality and smelling of drink should go unnoticed and unreproved . . .'

Soothed by his own rhetoric, and with the threat of the flowers removed, Cuthbertson felt for the moment quite in command of the situation. One of the things he enjoyed most was speaking at length without fear of contradiction.

Mafferty, for his part, seeing that the Principal's focus was on the far wall, and that his voice had settled at cruising speed, felt safe to relax the respectfulness of his posture somewhat, and allow his attention to wander. How strange the old boy had looked, clutching the flowers. Wild somehow, and at the same time, what was the word . . . *obedient*, like someone sleepwalking. He seemed normal enough now, though, going on about his bloody corporate enterprise. Corporate enterprise to line his own pockets. Who did the old fraud think he was taking in? The only place, the only kind of business, that appealed to mugs and crooks equally. One gigantic con. He is conning me now, or trying to. He is making a fortune through conning the students, half of whom are content to be conned and the other half preparing to con somebody else. An absolute winner. You can't go wrong. He thought again of the meeting with his friend Weekes, arranged for that evening. There was something in the wind, Weekes had said. Within a month they could be running their own business . . .

He looked with a sort of awe at Cuthbertson, who was still talking to the far wall in long fluent bursts marked by very brief pauses as if he were expertly gathering the next collocation before proceeding – an effect of scrupulosity reinforced by the almost startling punctilio of his clothing, immaculate dark suit, high stiff white collar, College of Further Studies tie, knotted exactly, perfectly symmetrical. Exactly symmetrical too was his position at the desk. He sat straight in his black leather chair, both thick shoulders at a level, pressed back against the back of the chair, head dead straight between them, elbows equidistant, hands – large, white hands, immaculate as to nails and half-moons – quite motionless on either side. Any slight movement he made seemed accompanied by a sort of caution, as if, Mafferty thought, he were balancing something on his head.

'I well remember,' he was saying now, 'my early days. My struggles, Mafferty.'

Becoming aware that he was once again being directly looked at, Mafferty sat forward and assumed an expression of alertness.

'I built this place up with my own hands,' Cuthbertson said.

'Did you really, sir?'

This simple question, which Mafferty had uttered merely because he felt some response was required, moved Cuthbertson, released that charge of emotion which was always near the surface when the School was under discussion.

'Yes,' he said, in suddenly vibrant tones, 'yes Mafferty, with my own hands. I believe in Free Enterprise, Mafferty. That is my personal creed. It was the creed of Hawkins and of Drake. I don't usually speak of it, but when I see a young fellow like yourself, in danger of going off the rails . . . This house, the whole place, was a ruin when I first saw it. To say that the garden was overrun would be an understatement. Flowers and weeds inextricably, ah, mingled. Shrubs growing everywhere unchecked. Windows warped and half the glass out. Door handles off.'

'Like a pioneer,' Mafferty said. He saw Cuthbertson's chestnut-coloured eyes through the glasses, big with the wonder of these recollections.

'Tramps had got in,' Cuthbertson said, 'and used the premises for their own insalubrious purposes. I won't enlarge on that. The house adjoins open country at the rear, as you probably know, and this open country was taking over. One of the first things I saw, on my initial tour of inspection, was a rat, a great brown fellow; it sat up and looked at me, Mafferty. The whole place was reverting to the wilds. It had become an embarrassment to the estate agents. But I saw the possibilities. I rose to the challenge. I believe in Free Enterprise, Mafferty, and that is how I see this School, as a monument to Free Enterprise in an age of gradually encroaching state control. It is a dramatic conception, and one that should unite and inspire us all, this course we are steering between nature in the raw and the ah, deadly uniformity of the State . . .'

With habitual envious fascination Mafferty embarked on the old familiar speculation. The fees varied of course, according to requirements; higher degrees came more expensive, but say seven hundred and fifty pounds, on average, for the twelve-week course, and say at any given time there were fifty or so students, that was in the region of thirty-eight thousand pounds, and multiply that by four . . .

'Like a pioneer,' he repeated, again meeting Cuthbertson's eyes.

'I beg your pardon?'

'A pioneer, sir.' Mafferty paused. Then, with a sense of brilliant improvization, he added, 'You know, opening up new frontiers.'

Cuthbertson was silent for some moments. Then he said, 'Yes, I accept that. But pioneers have to do more than achieve the conquest of nature, Mafferty, they have also to maintain standards. And that has been my great problem, to be frank with you, since we are having this confidential chat, and let me take this opportunity of saying how much I welcome these opportunities of getting to know my staff better, you must come and have supper with us one of these evenings so that we may have the opportunity . . .'

He fell silent again. One of his hands moved sideways along the desk, then back again. 'Where was I?' he said.

'Your great problem,' Mafferty said, thankful that he had been listening.

'Ah, yes, yes. My great problem, right from the start, has been how to reconcile the profit motive – I believe in the profit motive, Hawkins and Drake believed in the profit motive – with standards. To give, in short, value for money. That has been my slogan, right from the start. Value for Money. No one gets a degree here who has not fulfilled all our requirements.'

'I know that, sir, from my own brief experience here,' Mafferty said.

'We are not out of danger yet,' Cuthbertson said, raising his head. Light reflected from the large lenses of his glasses. 'I have had disquieting news lately, from reliable sources in the Ministry, and I won't disguise from you . . .'

Suddenly, in the midst of speech, he was attacked by discouragement and fatigue. He became aware of himself and Mafferty in the quiet office, two casual lumps of matter set in accidental proximity amid vacant wastes of air.

'If this attitude persists,' he said, 'we shall have to terminate what has been and could continue to be a fruitful relationship. Do you take my meaning?'

Startled by this change of tone, Mafferty sat forward. 'I think so, yes,' he said.

'We have no contract, as you know. And you have only been with me a matter of two months. I would not be required, in law, to give you much in the way of notice.'

'I realize that,' Mafferty said.

Cuthbertson's hand moved again, sideways and back. He felt blankness descending on him. The surfaces of his desk had shifting lights in them, like pools, shallow pools . . . He looked down at his memo-pad and saw the word 'Order'. That was it. With a great effort he began to speak again.

'I believe in order, Mr Mafferty. *Order*. By which I mean not so much discipline; that comes into it of course, but smooth running. *Smooth running*. Things working well, everyone pulling together, like a well-oiled machine, but with, ah, sentient cogs. Everyone seeing his way with absolute clarity, just as I see mine. That will be all, then, I think, for the moment.'

Exhausted, he watched Mafferty get up and walk away. It was eleven-thirty-two by the clock on the wall.

Baines was just entering the hospital. He had been dreading the visit, was only doing it from a stern sense of duty, to one of our brave boys, as he would have put it, wounded in action. Immediately on entering he felt oppressed, endangered. The smells and whiteness and long corridors and tubular equipment glimpsed here and there were like the concomitants of an ugly dream, and Baines was already in considerable perturbation of spirit before he got to Kenneth's ward. This was increased by the fact that the nurse on duty had to point Kenneth out to him – the lad was unrecognizable, bemonstered by bandages.

'Hello, old boy,' Baines said, with assumed heartiness, advancing towards Kenneth's bed, past a bed in which a very old man with a grey, bald, head sat staring straight before him, then another which was just a heap of bed-clothes, nothing human discernible.

'So here you are,' Baines said. Very little of the surface area of Kenneth's face was visible. The bandage supporting his jaw passed beneath his chin and was bound round the top of his head. Had that been all, it would have given Kenneth the look of a medieval knight in a white helmet; but, in addition to this, the left side of his face, which had sustained the damage, had a large dressing on it, extending from the corner of the mouth, almost where the helmet bandage ended, right up to the left temple, with a thick auxiliary strap completely covering the bridge of the nose.

His eyes looked out from this stiff white mask as if they had crept to the surface in order to signal.

'Well, you're not looking too bad,' Baines said. Conquering his aversion he looked steadily at Kenneth's bemonstered head. 'We shall have you up and out of here in no time . . . What did you say?'

Sounds had come from Kenneth, but curiously guttural and indistinct.

'I beg your pardon, old boy?' Baines said. 'I didn't quite catch that.'

Kenneth couldn't talk properly, he suddenly realized, because the bone structure of his face was rigidly strapped up and immovable; there was no play whatever in his lower jaw.

'Arree – shit arree mush,' Kenneth said. 'Tak allsh trull.'

'I didn't quite catch that,' Baines said again. Kenneth was being obliged to talk without moving his jaws at all, and this was producing a slurred monotone, very disturbing and disagreeable to Baines, for whom the effort of distinguishing a meaning in these guttural sounds now became part of the general horror of the place, the gleaming surfaces, and the smells, the all-pervasive smells of sickness and healing, the same smell to Baines, and a peculiarly repellent one. Sickness and unseemliness were intimately related in his mind, and he found it very difficult not to hold Kenneth accountable, morally, for his less than A.1 condition.

'What was that again?' he said, leaning forward and looking into Kenneth's dark, active eyes.

'Arree shit arree mush.'

'That's all right,' Baines said, nodding, bluffing, thinking how oddly dark and cavernous Kenneth's mouth looked against the white of the bandage.

'I'll tell you what,' he said. 'I'm going to see you have a citation for this; you are going to get the Order of Gallantry for it, old boy.'

Kenneth nodded slowly.

'I consider it a damn good show,' Baines said.

'Hankh – hoogh – arreghmush,' Kenneth said.

It must have been a hell of a whack, Baines thought. In half-darkness and a limited space, in the midst of brawling and stumbling and a confusion of bodies, someone had laid a loaded stick across Kenneth's face with what seemed absolute precision. For a moment or two his mind was occupied with a sense of this contrast, the precise, shattering blow amid that chaos, the instant tracery of fracture . . .

'Have you any idea – ' he was beginning, when there was an unearthly screech from one of the beds opposite. An emaciated person sat up suddenly and uttered a burst of high-pitched laughter towards the ceiling.

'Who's that?' Baines said. 'What – ?'

'Ersh sherraghich whurrd,' Kenneth said.

'What did you say?' Baines leaned forward again. It was warm in the ward and he felt himself beginning to sweat slightly. 'This is a ghastly place,' he said.

'Oh dear, oh dear,' a quavering querulous voice said, a few beds further down. 'Oh dear, oh my leg!'

'Sherraghuk whurrd,' Kenneth said again.

'Is there something wrong with his leg?' Baines started wildly in the direction of the voice. 'Do you mean geriatric? What, you mean they have put you in with the old people?'

He looked with horror at his lieutenant. 'But that is disgraceful,' he said. 'I'll see if I can get you moved.'

The white head moved from side to side, very slowly. 'Ishn't whurrsh ugh trull,' it said.

'You mean you don't mind?' Baines stared at Kenneth. He felt acutely uncomfortable. The sweat was running down his left side, inside his shirt.

'Oh dear, oh dear,' came again from the bed farther down, followed almost immediately by another screech of laughter from over the way.

'It's a madhouse,' Baines said. The smell of aged bodies and medicaments rose to his nostrils in suffocating waves. All his life he had hated age and deformity and people who were crazy or helpless or disabled. Such people made him feel sick.

'They should be put out of their misery,' he whispered vehemently, bringing his head closer to Kenneth's white helmet. 'As soon as people get too old and ah, I mean, reach a certain stage of infirmity, they should be put out of their misery.'

The heap in the bed next to Kenneth's moved suddenly.

'Deformed people, too,' Baines said, keeping his eyes on this heap. 'Why should we – ?'

'Hargh kark,' Kenneth said, moving his head cautiously up and down.

'What do you do with excrescences?'

An arm like a mildewed stick came groping out from the heap of clothes. Pyjama hung from it like the remnants of bark. It clawed briefly at the edge of a sheet.

Baines took out a large white handkerchief and wiped his sweating forehead and cheeks. 'You slice them off,' he said, close to Kenneth's white mask. 'You slice them, you slice their ballocks off, you . . . Metaphysically . . . A healthy society – '

'Arghee chorrcet-lurgh.'

'Functioning perfectly. Beautiful, vigorous bodies, disciplined minds. Like a beautiful machine with all its parts in perfect order. The day is coming and it is nearer than some of these anarchist shits think . . .'

'Ghaarloogh.'

5

Rousing himself with an effort from the torpor into which he had fallen after the interview with Mafferty, Cuthbertson decided to leave his office for one of his periodic tours – not of inspection, but of lonely communication with the spirit of the place. However, on opening his door, he found himself confronted by a tall thin figure in a cloth cap and white overalls holding something in its hand. His first reaction, as to anything unexpected these days, was a feeling of fear, intense enough to be momentarily disabling. But his senses cleared, and he made out pale features below the cap, saw it was a paint brush the person was holding, smelt fresh paint.

'What are you doing?' he said, in a passable imitation of his own voice. 'Are you painting?'

He found himself being regarded by very pale, vacant eyes. The man was quite young, little more than a youth, in fact. He said nothing, but gestured towards the door with his brush. Cuthbertson turned and looked. 'Ah,' he said, 'You are going to give my door a new coat of paint.' He looked for some moments longer at the gleaming, immaculate surface of his door. 'I don't think it needs one, actually,' he said.

The youth shook his head. Reaching past Cuthbertson, he pointed to the word 'Principal' painted in small black capitals on the door. Then he raised the paint brush above his lowered left hand.

'I see,' Cuthbertson said. 'You are going to make the letters bigger.' An idea of Bishop's, he thought immediately. He seemed to remember now having expressed in Bishop's hearing the wish that the word could be more boldly, more prominently displayed. Bishop was full of little ideas like this, rather touching little gestures of consideration. Surprises. It would be better, though, if he notified one, Cuthbertson felt.

He surveyed the painter doubtfully. Why did he not speak? He might possibly be dumb of course. None the worse for that *qua* painter, but there was something in the vacant eye, the ill-nourished elongation of the features, the uncouth silence, which did not inspire confidence. He did not strike Cuthbertson as a craftsman of the highest quality. Still, he must have passed through an apprenticeship of some kind.

'I suppose you've got stencils for the letters?' he said. A watery smile came to the youth's face, and he gestured again with the brush.

'Well,' Cuthbertson said, 'I suppose you know your own business best.' He moved past the youth and along the passage, still worried, however, at what he was leaving behind.

Distrust of the painter continued to nag him for some minutes longer as he moved around the School. He thought of checking with Bishop, then decided not to, on the principle of never appearing anything less than sanguine before subordinates – one of the cardinal rules of Leadership.

Gradually, as he proceeded, reaching out occasionally to touch with finger tips the smooth surface of wall or window sill, his qualms subsided, the familiar atmosphere of the School settled round him. He met no one in the corridors, as he padded noiselessly about. Everyone was in class at that hour of the morning.

He stood for some moments at a landing, looking out over the gardens behind the house, the neat lawns, trim alleys – that had been a marvellous idea, the intersecting box hedges, obliging the students to walk sedately during the breaks, precluding any possibility of horseplay ... Order and method, he thought. System, symmetry. A voice within him eagerly asserted, Yes, Donald, yes. This started up a dialogue which proceeded at an accelerating speed. A place for everything, everything in its place, place was a wilderness when you first saw it an embarrassment to the estate agents I built it up with my own hands a wilderness you saw the possibilities a rat sat up a big brown fellow looked at you me ...

Cuthbertson laid his forehead against the cool glass of the window. Words, voices receded. He rested thus for a while, then, when he felt calm again, continued on his way. Now and again he paused outside classroom doors, listening. Industrious silence, or the monologue of the teacher, came to him. The place was a regular hive, no other way of describing it. No small achievement, by one's own unaided efforts, to have created this great corporate enterprise dedicated to self-improvement. Once again he was surprised, almost awed, at the diversity within monumental unity that he had created, all these people going in their various ways about life's great business, the acquiring of qualifications . . . In classroom four, however, there seemed to be something of a rumpus going on. Voices were being raised in there.

Classroom Four was the one in which Mafferty was conducting his Literary Appreciation Class. He had been so shaken by Cuthbertson's threats of dismissal that he had gone over to the Black Lion immediately after the interview and had downed a couple of pints, much too quickly. Once in front of the class he had begun to feel the effects of this. Nevertheless, he had adhered to the hasty plan for the lesson, devised on the way back from the pub, and had written slowly and carefully on the blackboard:

> O rose, thou art sick!
> The invisible worm
> That flies in the night
> In the howling storm,
> Has found out thy bed
> Of crimson joy,
> And his dark secret love
> Does thy life destroy.

This done, he surveyed the class with a sort of glassy benignity, encountering as he did so the stern gaze of Mustapha, the Turk, in his accustomed corner, and the clerkly gleam of Hans beside him. Across from them, in the next row, he saw the fuzzy hive of Abdu and the dark Semitic face below it. There was a new student beside him, an elderly grey-haired man with a hearing aid, who looked like a northern European. In rapid review Mafferty took in the others: round-faced, small-featured Henry from Derby and beside him the other Englishman, Mr Butler, who rarely spoke and whose reasons for being there were obscure; in the desk behind them the gentle smile and silky moustache of Taba, from Iran; in the front row as usual, Javier, the keen Mexican.

For a moment or two Mafferty considered them in silence. The fact that his students desired to be instructed always puzzled him a little, perplexed his cynicism: they should only have been interested in obtaining what they had paid for, the certificate, the document; yet here they were, wanting to learn something.

'I want you,' he said, 'to read this short poem, and tell me what you think it means. It is a very well-known poem. I daresay you recognize it, Henry?'

Henry looked blinkingly at the board. His mental processes were very slow. 'Seen it before somewhere,' he said at last.

'It is by William Blake.' Mafferty arranged his face into an expression of academic shrewdness. 'I have chosen it,' he said, 'because it does exemplify what I've been saying to you lately about *meaning*. What do we actually *mean* by meaning? In poetic terms of course.'

He saw a frown of mingled displeasure and incomprehension on the face of Mustapha, and went on hastily, before the Turk could intervene with a question.

'This poem has a very, er, potent central symbol, one which we may disagree about, but I'm sure that whatever the disagreement in detail, what will finally emerge will . . . Well, perhaps you'd better all read it first.'

He sat down at his desk and rested his head in his hands. The room, which had originally been quite a large one, had been partitioned into two by Cuthbertson, in order to accommodate more students, and the material of the partitioning was not as soundproof as its designers had asserted. Beyond the partition Mr Binks was taking his Civics Class, a process which consisted in discussing some prominent feature of the day's news. In this interval of silence they all heard Mr Binks' high-pitched, deliberate voice through the partition, saying, 'We shall take as our subject today this latest bomb outrage.' There were some indeterminate sounds, feet moving, chairs scraping. Then Binks' voice came through again. 'No, I do not propose to discuss the arrangements for the Royal Wedding. Bombs are of more immediate concern than Royal Weddings.'

Mafferty looked up. He noticed at once with a preliminary, sinking feeling of boredom, that Taba, the most vocal member of the group, was regarding him with a sort of restrained, respectful eagerness. He delayed inviting Taba's answer for some minutes more, while they all listened to Binks, who was obviously reading from a newspaper:

The bomb, containing at least ten pounds of explosive, went off without warning just inside the main door. The front of the building was ripped apart. The room immediately adjoining, where some twenty people were drinking, was reduced to a crumpled wreckage of shattered furniture, glass and rubble, amidst which fragments of human bodies –

'Well, Taba?'

'This poem is, in my own opinion, one of corruption in the core,' Taba said, smiling gently. 'The rose is representing the whole of human condition and all our life when we are in the innocent conditions. The worm, it is knowledge?'

'Rubble?' they heard Binks saying. 'What means rubble? You should not say, "What means rubble?" You should say, "What does rubble mean?" '

'That is a very interesting interpretation,' Mafferty said, 'and one which – '

'The worm comes creeping and eats all up, so destroying the innocent conditions.'

'Yes, as I say, that is a most – '

'Excuse me, please, is wrong,' interjected Javier, moving his large head restlessly. He nearly always took issue with the Iranian; a sort of rivalry existed between them. 'Is quite wrong,' he said. 'Is a poem about the materialized society. All we care for is the goods, the merchandises, and that is why the poet he says our life destroy. Is not knowledge, as says Taba. Is the philosophy of Gross National Product.'

'Gross National Product?' Hans said, turning to the others in his stiff, courtly way. 'The Gross National Product does not mean nossing to William Blake.'

'You think I don' know heem, William Blake?' Javier demanded indignantly. 'I know heem.'

A doctor who lives only a few hundred yards from the scene of the explosion . . .

'You take the social and economic aspects,' Mafferty said, soothingly, 'as opposed to the moral. Well, it is a tenable point of view.' He glanced down at his watch. Still half an hour to go. He paused, wondering who to ask next.

. . . . most horrific sight of my life and I've seen a few in the past few years. Four of the people who had been flung out on to the pavement were clearly dead. One of them was just a torso . . .

'Well, Abdu?'

'Excuse please.' Mustapha raised a hand. 'What means "torso"?'

'You mean, "What does 'torso' mean?" '

'That is what I am asking *you*.' Mustapha said, with dignity.

'It is this part of the body,' Mafferty said, indicating. 'Now could we get back to the poem? What do you think, Abdu?'

'It is the Imperialist State,' the Libyan said, in his hoarse voice. Then he paused, looking round at the class, as if inviting approval, or exacting complete attentiveness before resuming.

'Yes, that's right, it is the trunk of the body. T-r-u-n-k, yes, that's it . . . No, I don't think we can call it a torso if there are arms and legs attached, certainly not if there are legs, no, the presence of legs would disqualify it from being a torso. As to arms . . .'

Hans sat up straight in his desk. 'I do not understand this word "torso",' he said. 'Is it including the head?'

'I think we should try not to listen to Mr Binks,' Mafferty said. 'It is this part of the body.' He again indicated. 'You have to be more specific if you want to include the head. You have to say "head and torso", but in this case, apparently, there was only the torso . . . What do you mean, exactly?' he said to the Libyan.

'The rose is imperialism,' Abdu said. 'And that is all corrupted by worms, the worms is the corrupting in the Imperialist State, which is a decadent one, because of exploiting the oil producers, for example. "Rose thou art sick" means England is sick because of exploitings going rotten now that the producers can put all their heads together and fix the prices. England is a decadent flower. Also, she is too much civilize.'

He glanced round again, his mass of tightly curly hair rising above the general level like a small dome on the skyline.

'. . . can't have a head,' Mr Binks said from the next room. 'No, definitely excludes the idea of a head . . .'

'That is basically what I would call a political – '

'Blake was interested in nature, wasn't he?'

'Well, Henry, all poets, practically all poets – '

'I don't mean only plants and that, but wild animals.'

'The area of a poet's likes is a pretty broad spectrum,' Mafferty said. 'But why "invisible"?' he said to Abdu, 'Why "*invisible worm*"?' He set his finger tips together in unconscious parody of Cuthbertson, and looked at his students over the bridge so formed.

I attended the wounded as best I could for an hour. It was difficult to know where to start. There were pieces and fragments of bodies . . .

Abdu shook his fuzzy head. 'Corrupting from the insides,' he said. 'Hopelessly roddled.'

'Riddled,' Mafferty said. 'Well, all these remarks have been very interesting and I think illuminating in certain respects – '

'It is a girl,' Mustapha said suddenly.

'I beg your pardon?'

' "Riddled"?' they heard Mr Binks say querulously. 'What means "riddled"? It means shot through with holes. Please try to ignore the sounds from Mr Mafferty's classroom.'

'I am in agreement with Abdu. It is a beautiful girl. Rose is the name of her.'

'He didn't quite say that, did he?'

'Your English rose, no?'

'Well,' Mafferty said doubtfully, 'I'm not sure whether that is really the interpretation I would have – '

'Excuse please, I am not saying that,' Abdu said, turning to look indignantly at Mustapha.

'Yes, yes,' Mustapha said, 'I am saying the same as you. She is the English rose that has got clapped. Else why it say about bed and secret love?'

In the weighty pause that followed upon this, they all heard Mr Binks say, ' "Clapped?" what means "clapped"? You mean, What does "clapped" mean? Or alternatively, what is the meaning of "clapped". It means "applauded". Now could we get back to – '

'Clapped?' Mafferty said. 'I don't quite see – '

'He said the same thing.' Mustapha pointed at Abdu. 'He said too much syphilis. That is the age-old problem of unlawful fornications.'

'It is not really a problem in this country,' Mafferty said. 'Actually. Very unpleasant of course, and all that, but with these new wonder drugs it is not the disaster it used to be.'

'Too much *civilize*,' Abdu said to Mustapha.

'What you say?'

'I did not say what you say, I say – '

'Excuse me please, what means "wonder drugs"?' Javier said, pencil poised between thick eager fingers.

'Penicillin, stuff like that,' Henry said.

'Antibiotics,' said Mr Butler, suddenly and loudly. 'The marvels of modern medical science.'

Perhaps because Mr Butler spoke so seldom, there was a little silence after this, during which they all heard Mr Binks saying, '. . . face blown off. Maimed? No, I don't think we can call having the face blown off the same as being *maimed*. I would call that disfigured rather than maimed. I would reserve the word maimed for – I beg your pardon? Mutilated? That is a good idea, Costas, yes, but wait a minute now, if you say *mutilated*, are you not implying that the surface of the face still remains, though badly damaged of course, whereas according to the newspaper account, this person had his face *blown off*. You must give due weight to the preposition . . .'

'In which this country has led the field,' Mr Butler said, as if there had been no pause whatever. 'You would still be biting on bullets and getting blotto on *raki* if it hadn't been for us,' he said looking across at Mustapha, who did not, however, pay him much attention, being still too occupied with his own interpretation of the poem.

'Not at the same time, surely,' Mafferty said.

'They sit here running us down,' Mr Butler said. 'This country has led the world in relieving pain and prolonging life.'

'Excuse please, what means "mutilated"?'

'They speak of beds and of dark love. Why they do that? That is not imperialism or society corrupting. That is extra-marital.'

'What means "maimed"?'

'It all demonstrates what we were saying last week,' Mafferty said, raising his voice, 'that a good poem, and it is possibly the test of a good poem, can be read on a number of different levels.' His head had begun to ache slightly. 'We can disagree as to detail,' he said, 'and yet we can be fully agreed as to the inherent, er, and that is possibly the real test of – '

'Civilize,' Abdu said, glaring at Mustapha.

Javier said slowly, 'It is a microcosmos of what is going on, you have not to see it only in the physical side.'

'Good point,' Mafferty said. 'Excellent point.' He glanced at his watch. Only three minutes to go. 'Perhaps,' he said, 'we could end by copying the poem, and then at home you could write a paragraph or so outlining your views on the meaning of it all . . .'

The yough engaged in painting Cuthbertson's door did not seem to have had any lunch break. When Cuthbertson returned, after his own modest sandwich, he was still at it, shoulders hunched forward in commendable concentration, brush held like a pen.

Cuthbertson paused benevolently. He was going through a phase of optimism and had quite forgotten his former distrust of the painter. The words, 'Ah, still at it?' were on his lips, to be delivered in a genial manner, when he noticed something terribly wrong with the lettering of 'Principal'. A disproportionately wide gap had been left between the 'r' and the 'i', and again between this and the following 'n'. Moreover, it was obvious to any impartial scrutiny that not enough space had been left for the 'pal' part, which the youth was embarking on now. The end of the word was thus certain to be marked by an undignified congestion. In short, it would have been difficult to imagine how anyone could have made a worse job of the lettering. This incompetent oaf had obviously failed to take into account the lesser bulk of the letter 'i'.

He had allotted too much space to it, then tried to put the matter right by leaving an equivalent space after it, with the result that the letter was isolated from the others, and stood out with an unnatural boldness. The word, and with it the concept, was made totally ridiculous by this loss of symmetry.

Cuthbertson stood still for a moment longer, jaws clenched. It was the arbitrary, absurd look of the word on the door, *his* door, his identity, that finally drove him, after this rigid pause, to furious utterance. He felt his face suffuse with blood. His eyes grew humid.

'What the devil,' he said, very loudly, 'do you think you are up to?'

These words, uttered with such angry emphasis, and from such close quarters had an electrifying effect on the painter, who did not seem to have been aware of Cuthbertson's presence until this moment. He started violently and turned, holding the brush breast high. His eyes stared wildly and a commotion set up in his adam's apple communicated to the corners of his mouth a series of twitches. He regarded Cuthbertson for some moments in this shocked goggling manner.

'I knew you would make a mess of it,' Cuthbertson said loudly. 'And do you know how I knew?'

The youth essayed a reply, but all that emerged was a series of gutterals interspersed with loud clicking noises.

'It was the arrogant way you reacted to my remarks about stencils.' Cuthbertson spoke more quietly, perceiving that the other had a speech defect. It was occurring to him, in any case, that this person was too poorly endowed all round to be a proper recipient for his wrath. Bishop, Bishop was the man. At this moment, as if called forth by the very urgency of his rage, Bishop appeared, hurrying towards them along the passage.

'I've just had the reply about Mafferty,' he said. 'He hasn't — '

'Never mind that,' Cuthbertson said in low, vibrant tones. 'Never mind that.'

'Is there anything wrong?' Bishop looked from Cuthbertson to the goggling painter. 'I thought I heard shouting,' he said.

Cuthbertson's cheeks began to tremble. At the sight of Bishop's face and the sound of his voice, an appalling rage began to possess

85

him. His vision was clouded, and he felt a dry constriction in the throat. The rage was like an ordeal, the effort to control it was an effort to survive.

'Have you seen this?' he said. 'Have you seen it?'

Bishop craned awkwardly, stretching his short neck to get a sight of the door, and this awkwardness of posture, so typical of him at any time, now acted as an extra irritant on Cuthbertson, who saw in his subordinate's ungainliness a sort of living proof of his ineptitude.

'Would you call that symmetrical?' Cuthbertson said. 'Would you call those letters evenly spaced?' Distinctly audible during the latter part of this question was the dry clicking of Cuthbertson's tongue against his rage-parched palate, a most unnerving sound, the more so as it reproduced on a smaller scale the characteristic effects of the painter's impediment, making this seem somehow infectious.

Bishop blinked at the door a moment longer. Then, perhaps to postpone meeting Cuthbertson's regard, he addressed himself to the painter. 'What's all this?' he said sternly. 'Is this the best you can do?'

The painter had not yet quite recovered from the shock Cuthbertson had given him. His eyes still had a wild look, and his mouth, though firmer now, stretched convulsively at the edges from time to time. He stared at them for a few moments, then uttered some words.

'What's that, what's that?' Bishop said, leaning forward in severe interrogation.

The youth spoke again.

'What does he say?' Cuthbertson demanded, licking dry lips. 'I can't make it out. The accent, I mean. Apart from anything else. He must be from another part of the country. Are – you – from – another – part – of – the – country?' he said to the youth, spacing the words out menacingly.

'What's that?' Bishop leaned forward again. 'Glamorganshire? He comes from Glamorganshire, Donald.'

'Ask him what he said before,' Cuthbertson said.

'Glamorganshire eh?' Bishop said. 'What did you say before? Before he asked you where you came from? What? No, before that, before Mr Cuthbertson asked you – '

'I cannot stand much more of this,' Cuthbertson said.

Bishop brought his face quite close to Cuthbertson's and said in low tones, 'He has a speech impediment.'

'Good God,' Cuthbertson said violently. 'Do you think – ' He was interrupted by a further series of sounds from the painter.

'He says it looks all right to him,' Bishop said, and stood alertly, waiting to relay a message back.

'Looks all right to him?' *Looks all right to him?* Ask him if he considers the word he has written on my door to be symmetrical, will you? Just ask him that simple question.'

'I doubt if the word is within his range,' Bishop said, 'I'll do my best.'

'Never mind,' Cuthbertson said loudly. 'It's no good blaming him.' The absurdity of the intermediary, interpretative role which Bishop was adopting added fuel to his rage.

'You have let the side down,' Bishop said to the painter. It was obvious that he was keen to stay on the side of outraged authority as long as possible. 'You have made a very serious blunder,' he said.

'No good blaming him,' repeated Cuthbertson, very loudly. 'The labourer is worthy of his hire. I blame you, Bishop. I hold you entirely responsible.' He was not aware of having chosen to speak so loudly. The volume of his voice seemed curiously arbitrary, as if decisions about it were being made elsewhere.

Bishop glanced around. Even at this moment of pressure, under fire as it were, he was concerned to protect the chief from the consequence of being overheard, the consequences of some student or member of staff seeing Mr Cuthbertson out of control like this.

Cuthbertson noticed the glance and understood it. He paused, breathing heavily. Then he said, 'We'd better go inside my office.' To the youth he said coldly, 'Just paint it over, will you? If that will not be taxing your skills too much.'

'I ought to have known,' he said, when they were inside the office. 'I ought to have known that something would go wrong with the enterprise.' He felt himself trembling in various parts of his anatomy, mainly in the area round his mouth, and behind his knees. 'I built this place up with my own hands,' he said.

'I know you did, Donald.'

'I saw the possibilities. I rose to the challenge.'

'Donald,' Bishop said, 'you are not looking at all well. Don't you think you ought to take one of those pills?'

Some weeks previously, when Cuthbertson's tensions had started to become severe, Bishop had persuaded him to go and see a doctor, who had prescribed tranquillizing tablets.

'Now?' Cuthbertson said. 'Barely two hours from the Degree Ceremony? With the Briefing Session to conduct before that? You know perfectly well that those pills have a stupefying effect on me.'

'I thought – '

'That is the trouble with you,' Cuthbertson said. The trembling behind his knees was increasing. He went round behind his desk and sat down. 'You never think things through,' he said. The ordeal of his rage had left him weak, not far from tears.

'By the way,' Bishop said, hoping by his news to avert further reproof, 'Mafferty – '

'That is all right, I have spoken to Mafferty. I don't think we'll have any more trouble on that score. No, you mean well, but you have a propensity to make a hash of things.'

Bishop stood in a position of respectful immobility, holding his hands at his sides. He seemed to be waiting, after this reprimand, for some N.C.O. to march him out.

'You were at a good school,' Cuthbertson said. 'You became a prefect in due course, or so at least you told me when applying for this post. You taught for some years at a prep school before coming here. You were in the Territorial Army.'

'Right on every count,' Bishop said, full of admiration at the Chief's grasp of detail.

'Such a course of life should have made you a shrewd judge of men, and I had always considered you in this light. A man used to appraising his fellows, making swift assessments of their worth and so forth. Yet you engage an obvious imbecile to paint my door, and to do that delicate and crucial lettering job.'

'He assured me he was up to it.'

'How could he possibly assure you of anything, with a delivery like that?'

88

'I think you may have startled him, Donald.'

'I hope you are not seeking to shift the blame?'

Bishop squared his shoulders and met his superior's gaze firmly. 'No, of course not,' he said. 'I accept full responsibility.'

'I should think so,' Cuthbertson said. This staunchness, which he thought of as truly British, was having its due effect. He was feeling steadier now, the trembling had passed. After some moments of uncertainty he suddenly experienced the triumphant sense of being about to embark on a speech. He placed his finger tips together, forming a bridge.

'It's not only that,' he said, 'but the slight to *me*, my authority. Think of it that way. There is more than just personalities at stake here. I am a symbol. I am both base and apex. I don't suppose you can readily conceive that, can you?'

'Well,' Bishop began, dutifully making the attempt, 'let me see now . . .' He made a line in the air with his forefinger and then with a prodding motion indicated a point above it. 'It is a spatio-temporal concept, isn't it?' he said.

'You cannot conceive it,' Cuthbertson said firmly, 'because it is inconceivable. Like alpha and omega, you know. Everthing depends on me. The whole structure of this small community of ours, this world in miniature, this little world of school. And there must be due order and proper government in every part, just as there must be in the world at large. I am the visible symbol of that order and government. I must be beyond repoach. I must be *seamless*. The smallest flaw in the design, the smallest suspicion that this or that was inadvertent, unforeseen, slipping out of control, this throws into discredit the whole structure, our world collapses. And the barbarian is always at the gate, never forget that.'

'Some of them have got in,' Bishop said, feeling bold enough now to venture a more joking tone, in spite of the Chief's strictures. He had, in any case, something in reserve, if things got sticky again, this bombshell about Mafferty – a sure way, whenever he chose to trot it out, of diverting the Chief's displeasure.

'Some of them are in our midst,' he said. 'Judging by the faces I see. There's a chap in Group Three who looks as if he'd be more at home with an assegai than a writing implement.'

'They need discipline,' Cuthbertson said. 'They need a touch of the spur, some of them. That is my whole point. Everything must seem to be intended. There is an overall design here. Everything has been foreseen, everything has been taken into account, from the interveiw procedures on the student's first arrival, to his graduation and translation to higher things twelve weeks later. Now if a student with some query not covered in the brochure and not dealt with in any of the various notices appearing on the notice board, if such a one – and he would already be a disaffected, potentially subversive person, since all possible queries are anticipated in one or the other of the ways I have mentioned – if he should find himself applying to my door and if the word 'Principal' on that door were grotesquely unsymmetrical . . .'

Cuthbertson paused and gave his Senior Tutor a meaning look.

'It might set him off on dangerous courses,' Bishop said.

'Exactly.'

'It might lead him to question our authority.'

'Quite so.'

Bishop felt he had hit a winning streak. 'It might – ' he began eagerly, but Cuthbertson had raised a hand.

'I see you have followed my reasoning,' he said. 'I realize you erred out of zeal. You must not think your devotion to the School goes unnoticed.'

'Thank you, sir.' Bishop felt a slight lump in his throat.

'Was it you, by the way, that put the flowers in here?'

'It was, yes.'

'Nice thought,' Cuthbertson said. 'Appreciate it. Had to get rid of them, though. They . . . distracted me.'

There was silence for a while, then Cuthbertson said slowly, 'I was perhaps a little hard on you, but I have had to be hard on myself lately.'

'How do you mean?' Bishop said, with immediate concern.

'Well, I have been a good deal troubled of late by doubts of various kinds.'

'Doubts?'

'Not, I hasten to add, doubts as to the value of what we are doing here.' Cuthbertson paused, looked in a cautious, almost

90

stealthy way at the clumsy attentiveness of Bishop's posture, the bemused loyalty of that florid face. The body of his Senior Tutor seemed to fall naturally into ungainliness. It was as if there were some private horror in Bishop at the implications of physical grace or elegance. However, he did not dwell on this thought, as it took him too close to Bishop's psyche, where he had no wish to be.

'I have never faltered in that,' he said. 'Never once. Not from the moment that big insolent brown fellow sat up and looked at me.'

'Big insolent brown fellow? Do you mean that chap from Haiti? What was his name now? Used to wear an earring, just one earring, in his — '

'I am referring to the rat,' Cuthbertson said, rather coldly.

'Rat?' Bishop raised a hand and laid it across the top of his head. His mind was a complete blank. Now was the time, he thought, to launch the bombshell about Mafferty, 'Speaking of rats — ' he began.

'Never mind, never mind.' Cuthbertson said. 'All I mean is, that it is not the value and importance of our work that I am doubting, but whether our standards are going to prevail. Some kind of element is creeping in, Bishop. There is a spirit abroad which I don't like.'

'Do you mean in the School?'

'I see it in the School. I see it in the world at large. A principle of disorder. An active principle. I am not talking about disorder by default or neglect. I am referring to the ancient evil of anarchy.'

'We must fight it,' Bishop said.

Cuthbertson's head had begun to ache again, rather badly. 'I don't know what to do about it,' he said. 'My mind seems to get very clouded these days. Personal issues seem to intrude. The past, matters from the past, come into my mind in the most extra-ordinary way. I don't quite know how to describe it — they seem to take up all the space. Lately it has been some daffodils I once gave to my wife.'

'Daffodils? You need a rest, Donald. It is a very long time since you had a holiday.'

'H'm, yes.' Cuthbertson nodded, cunningly pretending to

believe that the School could function in his absence. There were some things too burdensome for Bishop to know.

'I don't want to add to your troubles,' Bishop said. 'But I'm afraid we've had a negative response to our enquiries about Mafferty.'

'What do you mean?'

'Trinity College, Cambridge, have no record of any such person.'

'You mean he has no degree from there?'

'He does not seem to have ever been a member of the student body.'

'My God,' Cuthbertson said. 'He has been deceiving us all this time. He has been posing as a graduate. Why wasn't this known before? I remember quite distinctly sending you a memo on the subject.'

'It took them some time to go through their records,' Bishop said, glancing down at his feet. He would not for worlds have told the Principal that his handwriting had been deteriorating for weeks, was now so illegible that no one any longer made any serious attempt to read it. He himself did his best to interecept as many of Cuthbertson's notes and memoranda as possible, in an effort to keep the knowledge of this deterioration from spreading.

'My God,' Cuthbertson said again. 'The deceit of it. The sheer, barefaced deceit of it.' He was much too disturbed by the news to go further into the reasons for the delay. 'I think we both need a drink,' he said.

He opened a drawer low down in his desk, took out a half bottle of brandy and two glasses. 'For medicinal purposes,' he said, pouring out.

'Here's to the School,' Bishop said. '*Semper floreat.*' He felt the need for a drink after this monumental wigging he had received from the chief. He had really been hauled over the carpet. He had deserved it too, no doubt about that. Richly. He opened his mouth to let the fiery breath emerge.

'I knew all the time there was something wrong with that fellow,' Cuthbertson said. 'I've got a shrewd instinct in these matters. No dedication, no idealism. That was my diagnosis. I made allowances, on the grounds that a chap with a degree from

Trinity College, Cambridge, can't be all bad. Now I find there is not even this to be urged in mitigation. For two months he has been standing before our students, without a qualification. Think of the harm he may have done.'

'I could boot the fellow all round the garden,' Bishop said. 'Gladly. It's times like this that I really feel sorry we don't have conscription any more. Six weeks square-bashing would do fellows like that a world of good.'

'Think of the sheer moral baseness of it,' Cuthbertson said. 'Claiming to have a degree and not in fact having one. He didn't even follow a course there, which makes the whole thing more heinous.'

'The fellow's a real *anguis in herba*, no doubt about that,' Bishop said.

'He'll have to go, of course.'

'Of course.'

'The sooner the better. I'll speak to him after the Briefing Session.'

'Are you going to let him attend the Degree Ceremony?'

'Well, I don't want to be too hard on him,' Cuthbertson said. 'After all, it will be his last. And who knows, perhaps he will realize, even at this late stage, as he sees the students going proudly up to receive the degrees they have earned, perhaps he will finally understand that there are no short cuts in this life, you get nowhere without hard work and self-discipline.'

6

After lunch, quite suddenly, the sky clouded over, and a light rain began to fall. It was still raining as Lavinia set out the tea-things for herself and Mr Honeyball. She glanced from time to time out of the window at the garden, where the soft heedless rain went on falling, slanting down between the alleys formed by the low hedges, on to the grass. No wind, she noticed: leaf and flower hung motionless, passive before the rain. Would Mr Honeyball be late? In her pleasurable excitement she visualized him as he would arrive, stepping along the wet paving stones to the door, his narrow shoes gleaming, lightly stepping, his thin pale face and rimless glasses questing alertly, in his hand a slim black briefcase with gilt fittings and clasps. She thought of his meticulous moustache, two narrow slanting lines of dark brown hair, like Ronald Colman's. It was a sophisticated moustache, and below it Mr Honeyball's mouth was compressed, patient.

She switched on the radio and like an omen of successful consummation it was one of the old-timers, David Lovejoy, just starting to sing 'Dangerous Midnight'. Lavinia joined in eagerly, in her slightly clotted soprano, as she moved here and there, setting all in readiness.

Mr Honeyball was not a stranger, exactly, he had visited the school several times in his capacity of Ministry of Education official, three times in the last month, in fact. Donald of course was worried by this; he didn't like this interest on the part of the Ministry, something about a take-over, but why should the State be interested in a little place like theirs? No, she thought she knew why Mr Honeyball came so frequently, and it had nothing to do with his official function. He came in need. So while not technically a stranger, in the world of romance he was one; in that rainbow-tinted, many-splendoured zone he could be regarded as such, as someone who might suddenly, fulminatingly, be glimpsed among indifferent faces, who might declare himself, and this might happen now, today, because this world of love was a completely different world, where everything began anew.

Cups, saucers, bowl, jug were all deep blue stoneware. Spoon and tongs silver. On the low rectangular pine table the whole ensemble looked tasteful. 'Borrowed love, stolen kisses, da-dee-da-dee-da.' David Lovejoy, there was a man for you, none of your unisex persons, tight trousers but what was there inside them? No, not one of that lot. She liked a man who was a real man. Mr Honeyball was slender, he was a different sort, more of a brain worker, but there was a clench and pounce about him, that neatness was fierce, she thought. He could be in one of those films you saw, in some tropical corner of empire. When we had the empire. Not giving in for one second, either to the debilitating climate or the lax ways of the natives. Yearning inside, of course. Repressed and malarial. And so sexy and steamy out there in the bush, on safari, or tea-planting, or one of those Forgotten Men in the French Foreign Legion. Always dress for dinner, and so forth. Well, that was the British way. But my God, she thought, how their sheer appetite must build up over the weeks and months, all pent up inside them. Boundless ambitions possessed Lavinia suddenly. She wished she could multiply herself to satisfy all that need, bear the white men's burden, patrol the skies like Super-woman, zooming down on desperate men. Mr Honeyball at least she could get to. He has that walk, she thought, as if it were all accumulated inside him, that tense, rather jerky way of walking, the feet flicking outwards, a gait absolutely redolent of sexual energy. There was a lot in the way men walked. Donald had a padding obedient walk, as if he were answering some call . . .

Well, here she was, perfumed and prepared, ready and willing to assuage Mr Honeyball, turn him into a sated stroller, if only they could get on to those terms. That had been the problem hitherto; things had been kept too formal, too much at a conversational level, with Mr Honeyball shy and neat, not allowing himself to relax even, let alone unbutton. This time, Lavinia had decided, things would be taken a stage further. 'Once you have found him never let him go.' A deep-chested man, David Lovejoy. He was a long-distance lorry driver before his leap to fame.

She checked the tea-things once again, while the voice of the former lorry-driver continued, full of power and yearning, announcing the miraculous dream come true, the disappointments of the years expunged, all dross purged in that moment of recognition, and a perfect sexual union to follow, transport upon transport and throe upon throe until the shudders of the last trump. That was the message and he was putting it over well.

Lavinia found herself entirely in accord. That sudden blinding moment that redeems all had been taken for granted since her earliest girlhood, the possibility of it implicit in practically all she had read since then. The words she was listening to, the swirling sweetness of the accompanying strings, were not bemoaning a void but signalling faith in the possibilities of life. On some enchanted occasion one stood before another person and *knew*. This simple faith had survived all conjugal disillusionment, all knowledge of her own carnality. It was as vigorous now, this warm rainy afternoon, as she set out the tea-things, as it had ever been.

On a large, curly-edged plate, blue and white, with a pattern of mandarins and dwarf trees, she laid out the sandwiches, some egg, some ham. She had trimmed off the crusts for the sake of elegance – Mr Honeyball, she had observed, was not by any means a gross feeder, whatever the degree of relish. Around this centre-piece were smaller plates, bearing eclairs, meringues, small amenable doughnuts. Everything was in readiness. David Lovejoy ended on a high note. The music throbbed into silence. A diffident voice with a northern accent spoke briefly of next day's weather, predicting that it would be unsettled. This was succeeded by another voice, which said, rather sternly, *Here are the news headlines: One more victim of last night's bomb outrage has died in hospital, bringing the total of deaths to twenty-four. The Prime Minister and leaders of the Opposition are due to meet one hour from now to discuss the possibility of forming a Government of National Unity. No statement of the agenda has yet been released, but the Prime Minister himself is expected to make a brief statement after the meeting. Reports still coming in from Bangladesh speak of widespread –*

Pouting with boredom and disgust Lavinia switched the set off.

In the Home for Aged Gentlewomen, Mrs Mercer and Mrs Greenepad were listening to the radio too, the latter to the very same news bulletin that had so disgusted Lavinia, the former to ballet music. They each had their own set now: the radio ordered for Mrs Mercer by Lavinia had been delivered some ten minutes previously; and after a brief impromptu dance of delight by the old lady, in which hair-pins and exclamations had been shed all over her side of the room, it had been at once turned on. Now the two old ladies were sitting at opposite ends of the room, each listening with a harassed expression to her own set, each doing her level best to ignore the sounds emerging from the other. Mrs Greenepad, as was her wont, was listening to the news, for pleasurable confirmation that things were falling apart; Mrs Mercer had decided to celebrate her new-found independence by listening to a concert by the B.B.C. Northern Orchestra, leader Paul Beard, which was at present playing Prokofiev's overture to *Romeo and Juliet*. Neither of the old ladies was able to enjoy her chosen programme because of the distraction caused by the other. And this distraction was increasing, because each of them kept raising the volume.

Who actually started it was destined to be a source of acrimonious discussion for a long time to come, but Mrs Greenepad was probably the aggressor. Old as she was, long accustomed to unquestioned supremacy and sole control of all transmissions she did not at first fully appreciate the challenge. She had reacted quite uncompromisingly to the swirling of the ballet music by giving her volume control a quarter turn. Her room-mate, determined, after the long years of deprivation, to assert herself, had promptly done the same. Ballet music at a loud volume has a very sinister, threatening sound, and she was beginning to feel frightened, but she was resolved not to give in.

It now seems clear, Mrs Greenepad's announcer said stridently, *that the Town Criers are not the group responsible for the latest bomb outrages. Of the remaining claimants the most likely would appear to be –*

Mrs Greenepad, though listening intently, failed to hear the name of the terrorist organization concerned and, in annoyance at this failure, which she attributed to her room-mate's having turned her set up again, she gave her volume control another quarter turn. At this volume the voice of the announcer was distorted; the moment had been reached when any further build-up would be counter-productive. Mrs Mercer, aware of increased blare from behind her, escalated in her turn – too much, because her hands were trembling, and clumsy in their movements. The music was now thunderous. Mercutio was being slain under circumstances damaging to the eardrums, cymbals crashing and ripping through bull roar of bassoons, drums pounding like Mrs Mercer's own heartbeats madly amplified. She was badly frightened now and felt a sensation of being drawn in, engulfed in that fury of sound. But she persisted, not really any longer by an effort of will, but because she felt bound to the wheel, and must endure. With the tiny part of her brain not blasted and numbed by the sound, she obliged her head and right hand to move in palsied time to the music, in an attempt to bluff Emily, convey an impression of insouciance.

. . . .*reported earlier to have lost an arm, has merely suffered the loss of thumb and forefinger on his right hand. In some cases, owing to extensive facial injuries, identification has not been possible. The Archbishop of Canterbury has described the explosion as an outrage.*

About time, about time, Mrs Greenepad thought wildly. About time the church took a hand. The music had subsided considerably. Mrs Greenepad, not knowing this was merely to mark the expiry of Mercutio, and assuming it to be a concession on the enemy's part, lowered her own set by a quarter turn. Almost at once the music gathered strength again, adequately to represent Romeo's guilt and rage.

This rage of Romeo's coincided with Mrs Greenepad's at what she imagined to be Edwina's perverse refusal to compromise. She turned up her own set even louder than before, to its maximum in fact. The announcer's voice now became extremely difficult to make out, so great was the distortion. He was yelling as if he had himself begun to suffer some of the agony he described daily.

. . . vultures grey and evil, bellowed the announcer. *Dead children wrapped up in* – Plasticine? No. Polythene, probably. Aha! Mrs Greenepad screamed to herself. Where did they get the polythene from? *Her gender has not so far been revealed to the press, but a statement* – Her gender? That couldn't be right . . . The music had now got inextricably mingled with the news, forming a crashing, swirling accompaniment to the boom of the words. Mrs Greenepad twisted round furiously, saw her room-mate still bravely nodding her dishevelled head to the music. She was unable, however, to see the expression of terror on Edwina's face . . .

'I'll turn mine down, if you will,' she screamed at the jigging head.

Mrs Mercer gave no sign. She had not heard. Suddenly a furious knocking began on the right hand wall, as if someone were striking against it with a heavy object. Mrs Oakley from next door. She would be coming in next. No interference, Mrs Greenepad thought dazedly. We'll fight this out for ourselves. Her eyes and the whole top part of her head were throbbing painfuliy. She got up, went to the door, resisted the temptation to open it and escape, bolted it, returned to her booming set.

Mrs Mercer saw nothing of this action. She had not heard the knocking either, or if she had, had assumed it to be some activity of the drums. Romeo was on the point of putting paid to Tybalt. She was shudderingly attached to her set now, by some terrible current which would not release her. Her mouth was open, her eyes were glazed, the jigging of her head had become quite involuntary.

The man, thought to be an Indian, took a – Bakshish? Backseat? *He told the driver* – Taxi . . . *Indian youth told the driver . . . burial crowd, ground . . . thought the man . . . funeral. Carrying a suit* chased? *case . . . driver what appeared to be the body of a child . . . white darling. Darling? Towelling . . . Wrapped up in white towelling . . .*

'Turn your set down,' screamed Mrs Greenepad. Mrs Mercer did not hear her. There was a violent knocking at the door. Mrs Greenepad's set emitted a fizzing sound, then a loud pop, and fell silent. An acrid smell of burning filled the room. Mrs Mercer, aware of the sudden cessation of sound behind her, made a great effort and with trembling hands, too dazed to feel triumph, turned her set off.

The Briefing Session was held in a long, narrow room with a highly polished rectangular table going down the middle. This room was known as the Committee Room, and used by Cuthbertson for all gatherings of staff. He was sitting in his customary position now, at the head of the table with Bishop on his right. On the wall behind him was a full-length portrait of a man in mortar-board and gown, standing in a pose of affable dignity, holding in his hands a scroll. This was a portrait of Cuthbertson in his capacity as Founder.

Now, about to set things in motion, he looked with a certain wariness at the little group of waiting faces. My staff. He felt for the moment no power to utter words that might be to the purpose. The water carafes and glasses gleamed along the table, well polished, he noticed, and properly set out. Bishop's doing . . . The glasses were reflected in little pools along the surface of the table.

'Is everybody present?' Cuthbertson said.

'I believe so, yes, Mr Cuthbertson,' Bishop said deferentially. He never used his first-name privilege when there were others present.

'Ah,' Cuthbertson said, then paused, his attention again helplessly trapped among the reflections from the glasses, gleaming yet firm-edged, a series of precisely delimited pools of light. The bay below possessed precisely this quality of pallid radiance. But the room itself was blanched, shadowless. The throats of the daffodils deep yellow, clamorous . . . Somebody down the table spoke in a low voice. Feet shifted. Bishop shuffled papers, glancing about. The phone on Cuthbertson's right rang suddenly, starling everyone. Cuthbertson picked up the receiver, inclined his head to it – he had a curiously suppliant way of speaking into the telephone.

'Yes,' he said. 'Yes?' For some moments he could not understand what the call was about, then he realized that it was his secretary, speaking about a plumber who had just arrived. Cuthbertson's mind cleared. He remembered the insidious, the impermissible dripping of the bathroom tap. A man had come to repair it. 'Yes,' he said. 'Show him straight up to the bathroom, will you, Miss Naylor?'

He replaced the phone, cleared his throat, and raised his face in a blind but dominating manner. 'There are one or two things,' he said slowly, 'that I wish to bring to your attention, particularly as regards the ceremony this afternoon. By the way, I'd like a word with you, Mr Mafferty, when this Briefing Session is over.'

'Right you are,' Mafferty said.

'It is the ceremony later this afternoon,' Cuthbertson said, transferring his gaze from Mafferty with something of an effort, 'that I want to talk to you all about. I am particularly anxious that everything should go smoothly. Last time there were not enough chairs provided.' He looked at Bishop, who nodded and wrote something down.

'That's the kind of thing that gets us into a bad odour,' Cuthbertson said. He looked down at the paper before him. 'There are twenty-five students receiving the B.A., fifteen receiving the B.Sc., three M.A's, two Ph.D's and one Professor Emeritus – that is Mr Austin, who in my opinion has a brilliant future before him.'

'Hear, hear,' Bishop said. 'A first-class brain.'

'All these students are paid-up, all have attended regularly and applied themselves. I should like the ceremony to be conducted with dignity and decorum. I should like all the staff to wear their gowns. You have gowns, I issued you with gowns, so there is no excuse for not wearing them. Last time a member of staff appeared in a polo-neck sweater. Many of our students are from the emergent nations, I hardly need to remind you of that, and I should like them to carry away with them a proper sense of our older established civilization, the way we do things here, in the old country.'

'The old firm,' Bishop said.

Cuthbertson paused, looking at his second-in-command. 'I don't want anything to miscarry this time,' he said.

'Quite so,' Bishop said, continuing to make notes.

'It is their crowning moment, remember that,' Cuthbertson said. 'Walking up to the platform, the Union Jack draped over the table, shaking hands with me, the Principal, receiving their hard-earned qualifications amidst the plaudits of their fellows . . .'

He looked from face to face, launched at last, his eyes humid behind the glasses. None of the teachers quite met his gaze.

Lavinia went over to the large oval mirror on the wall, and surveyed herself, holding her face at various angles to the glass so that the light would fall on it in different ways, and she could check that her make-up was evenly applied, no tell-tale smears or blobs, no inexplicable suffusions, no hint of the hectic.

She saw nothing amiss. Her eyes were bright, her face had the composure of recently made-up faces. Her dress too she thought suitable to the occasion, white linen, very thin, indeed partially diaphanous, square at the neck in peasant style, and cut very low. She was wearing a bra of daring design, which drew her breasts together while actually containing only the lower halves of them.

She spent some time practising in front of the mirror, rehearsing poses that might be employed while entertaining Mr Honeyball. She thrust her shoulders back and raised her head mirthfully, thus forcing her breasts forward and causing the naked nipples delectably to press and prick against the thin material of her dress. That might be an appropriate response to any little witticism Mr Honeyball might utter. Alternatively, by leaning forward, as one might in offering a sandwich, she exposed her cleavage, a deep, smooth, creamy-white cleft. She had always, from a girl, had this creamy, satiny skin, absolutely flawless, all over her body.

She was heartened and encouraged by these exercises. When she could think of nothing else to do she dabbed a little more scent on her bosom and throat. She waited. She thought for a while about being forty, and about the people who were coming to her fancy-dress party that evening. Then she thought about Walter, their former gardener. He was a tall young man with reddish hair and pale blue eyes and a habit of whistling to himself as he went about his work, but his distinguishing feature, and one she had been quick to discern, was an imbalance in his trouser front, indicative of permanent semi-erection. How Donald, with his passion for symmetry, could have engaged a gardener with a permanent bulge on the left side of his trouser front had always been something of a mystery.

One day, in early spring, tulip-time, we had been married five years that March . . . pleasurably Lavinia embarked upon the familiar narrative. By dint of going over the incident in her mind she had shaped it into a gossipy sort of anecdote. I was telling him, telling Walter, my plans for the herbaceous borders. I had this idea of lupins, all different coloured lupins, massed together down the centres, lovely flowers, so *English*, and pansies at the edges. With pansies and lupins you couldn't want for colour, could you? Maybe some of those French marigolds mixed in. I like a show, I like a good show of colour. I was explaining this to Walter when he suddenly put a hand on the small of my back. Some force outside myself made me go right on talking. If I had allowed a silence to develop, I don't think he would have had the strength of character to proceed. I went right on talking. I was telling him to bank up the earth in the middle, to get a nice sloping effect, when he started pushing me along towards the tool-shed. He kept saying 'Yes, ma'am,' just as if nothing was happening, and I went right on talking about the herbaceous borders. All the time we were walking to the toolshed, a distance of some fifteen yards I was going on telling Walter that I wanted the flowers in ranks, I wanted a tiered effect, so it was important to . . . 'Yes,' he said, 'Yes ma'am.' He put me up against the back of the toolshed. Don't forget, I said, I want lupins, don't you go putting gladioli in. The buckle of his belt hurt my stomach, and that was the only thing of a personal nature I said to him then or ever, you'll have to remove your belt, I said, and he did so. He had me standing up against the toolshed. I was fully clothed except for my knickers; those he took off. I was still going on about the lupins, though by this time finding it difficult to control my breathing. I couldn't stop, I thought it might break the spell, as if somehow it was all the talk of herbaceous borders that had inflamed Walter in the first place and was now adding fuel to his libido. I was still trying to tell him about the lupins while he was actually . . . I've never been able to view lupins since in quite the same way. It was *lovely*.

Lavinia pressed hands against hot cheeks. She did not want to look red. Mr Honeyball would be here soon.

The plumber's name was Adams. He was a stoutish, thick-necked, censorious man in early middle age, with a high colour and a more or less permanent look of indignation. This deepened as he was shown up to the bathroom by Miss Naylor whose mini-skirt, preceding him up the stairs, revealed practically all there was of her shapely, silk-clad legs. The lubricity aroused in Mr Adams by this sight was at once, by some chemical change, converted into disapproval, he being a man whose impulses and passions had over the years got hopelessly mixed up with the habit of denigration; so much so that a sort of instantaneous trans-ference was effected whenever, as now, he was vouchsafed more than his usual visual ration of the female form. He followed the secretary's legs up the stairs, lusting and disapproving in equal measure.

His sense of Miss Naylor's brazenness was reinforced by the luxurious softness of the carpeting under his heavy shoes, and by the obvious expensiveness of all the fittings and furnishings that met his view. He hoisted his bag of tools, looking grimly upwards at the backs of Miss Naylor's thighs. He noted red-shaded wall lamps on the landing. Call this place a school? Not on your nelly. He was a reader of the Sunday Press, he knew about dens of vice. This was a high-class *bordello*. Plenty of money about. Not short of a bob or two. Probably cost you a week's wages just for a quick bash. The thought envenomed his already strong feelings of disapprobation. When the revolution comes, he thought, the *real* revolution, we'll clean up places like this, vicious smears on our civilization, and make sure we get fair shares for all . . .

He followed the secretary along a passage, past a picture of wild horses tossing their manes, past a number of closed doors. A tall pale man passed them silently, with a sidelong glance from prominent, yellowish eyes.

'Who was that, then?' Mr Adams said, drawing alongside the secretary. 'One of your clients, was it?'

'A student,' Miss Naylor said. 'From the Middle East.'

Pull the other one, Mr Adams thought. That man had a sated look. Bloody foreigners, coming here, taking advantage of the fall in the pound.

'Oh, yes?' he said, in a tone that conveyed disbelief.

'Here we are,' Miss Naylor said, opening a door. She preceded him into the pink and black bathroom. 'It is the hot-water tap on the bath,' she said.

Mr Adams had been further offended by the colour-scheme. He looked at the tap, which dripped steadily and obviously into the bath. The sight of it confirmed his unfavourable opinion of the place. People who admitted openly to faults in their water-systems he regarded with suspicion anyway. Any man not hopelessly corrupt would have rolled his sleeves up and had a go at this himself. 'I would not of known that,' he said.

'What?'

'That it was the tap. I might of spent the whole afternoon searching out the trouble.'

His sarcasm effected no change in Miss Naylor's features. 'You'll be all right, then, will you?' she said, lingering at the door, touching her hair with silver-tipped fingers.

'All right?' Mr Adams said, looking at her with his habitual indignation. 'Yes, I should think I'll be all right here. I can always have a wash and brush-up, if I come to the end of my resources, like.'

Miss Naylor turned indifferently away and disappeared through the door. Mr Adams' face relaxed with sour satisfaction. That had put her in her place a bit, he thought. Showing off her arse like that. Probably one of the call-girls, if the truth was known. He turned and regarded the offending tap.

'Leave it to me,' Bishop said, busily writing. 'Leave it to me. Have no fears about the seating arrangements.'

'If there is nowhere to sit,' Cuthbertson said, 'they might move about, start congregating in groups. You see the dangers?'

'Discipline, they lack discipline,' Bishop said. 'That is what they are deficient in. You can't blame them. They haven't had the benefit of our institutions. That sort of discipline and self-control – why, it takes generations to produce that.'

'We can impart something of it,' Cuthbertson said. 'We can sow the seed. I am just an old-fashioned patriot, really. People say this country's voice no longer carries the same weight, that we are no longer pre-eminent in the councils of the world. And this may be true in a temporary sense. But one thing we have got, something that can't be taken away from us, something that doesn't depend on overseas possessions or military power, and that is moral influence. *Moral influence.* The influence of our great past, our civilized standards. These graduates of ours go forth to the four corners of the earth, bearing our standards, to make a play on words . . .'

'Ha, ha,' Mafferty said, anxious to get into the Principal's good books again.

Cuthbertson regarded him without expression.

'It is a great thought,' Bishop said, also looking at Mafferty.

'To take one example,' Cuthbertson said, 'among many. There is a delegation from Turkey due to arrive later this afternoon. These are people interested in, ah, founding private universities in their own country. They come to us for guidance. I shall be showing them round. They will form certain impressions. That is what I mean by moral influence. It is a great trust.'

His eyes as he spoke were on Mafferty, who did not feel comfortable under this regard but tried to gain ground by nodding earnestly and repeatedly.

'Well,' Cuthbertson said, and once again it was something of an effort to look away from Mafferty's nodding face, 'before we break up . . . You have no further business, Mr Bishop?'

Bishop shook his head, pushing out his lips in the judicious pouting expression he used to denote complete mastery of a situation.

'There are one or two things I should like to say,' Cuthbertson said. He cleared his throat and reared up his head until his neck was at its fullest stretch. 'If I could revert,' he said, 'briefly, to the presentation ceremony due later this afternoon . . .' He paused. There was nothing, really, to say. Everything had been gone into, every detail planned. The ceremony would follow the usual procedure. But he wanted the reassurance of feeling that his staff was behind him, on this important occasion.

'We are only as strong,' he said, 'as our weakest member. I would like you to remember that. I want to feel that you are behind me, to a man. "United we fall, divided we stand." No, wait a minute, I've got it wrong.'

The slip routed him completely. He looked from face to face, attempting laughter. 'It's the other way round,' he said. 'Divided we *fall*.' The blood beat in his temples. The faces of his staff began to caricature themselves before his eyes. All their expressions seemed slowly to intensify, as if in this wilful manner they were hinting at hidden, more profound divisions. Bishop's face furrowed deeper in the travail of pointless, unproductive cerebration; Beazely's sagged with bland self-complacence; Binks' grew sharper-nosed, more acquisitive. All, all of them grew momently more hideously themselves.

The sense of danger, dreadful danger, returned to Cuthbertson; the certainty that these people, like all groups, were a threat to peace and order, unless they could be controlled, dominated, organized. He closed his eyes for a moment. Into his dazed and almost paralysed mind there came the vision of Bishop as he had stood that morning awaiting orders: jacket; white collar and plain tie; fawn trousers; suede footgear. He opened his eyes again. It struck him suddenly, with immense force, what a motley crew his staff was, all so differently attired.

'Well,' Bishop said, regarding the chief anxiously, 'if there is no further business, we could perhaps – '

'One moment,' Cuthbertson said loudly. 'Just one moment.' There was deep silence in the room. The surface of the table continued to deploy its tricky pools of light. 'What I must insist on is standards,' Cuthbertson said. Dimly, beyond the barriers of the present he glimpsed a possible state of being for himself, longed for and dreaded, destructive freedom, violent peace, paradoxes that his mind sheered away from.

'Standards,' he said. 'All around us, on every side, there are the foes to civilization, those who would undermine our standards, there are people and ideas whose very existence is a threat to the social fabric. And I am using that term in the very widest possible sense . . .' It seemed to him as he spoke that his words were forming the only track in a wilderness of silence. So long as he went on talking there was a way to follow. At the outer edges of his words vast deserts of silence began. This slender track of speech was threatened at every smallest pause by thick drifts of silence. In the effort to prevent this obliteration he found himself talking faster and faster . . . 'Academic standards, the highest possible critical standards, such as I like to think we enforce here, in this, ah, enclave, but there are other standards too, standards of *dress*, I often feel *besieged* as I go about my work here, yes, it is the only word, besieged by these forces militating against standards, you did not know that while you are teaching I am constantly patrolling, did you, no, you didn't know that, yes, I maintain an unremitting vigilance, yes, it is the only word, I often feel that the smallest relaxation on my part would result in engulfment, and that is what I want of you that you continue to give me your support, help with the sandbags, of course, I speak meta-phorically . . .'

Cuthbertson laid a hand on his heart in a dramatic gesture very unusual with him. He was breathing heavily, and his eyes behind the heavy glasses were wide and staring. Once more, like pain gathering, he felt the possibility of violence and freedom. 'Give me your loyalty,' he said. 'The least you can do. Loyalty to *me*. *To me*. I would like to see male members of staff dressed as follows: dark jacket or blazer, white shirt, tie of a plain colour. I do not specify the colour . . .'

'More tea?' Lavinia said tenderly, rising and holding out her hand for Mr Honeyball's cup, remembering to lean towards him at the same time, with her left elbow tucked well into her side.

'Ah, thank you.' Honeyball handed over his cup with a pinched white smile. He had been from the start both flattered and alarmed by the emphatic hospitality Mrs Cuthbertson had displayed towards him. He took out a white handkerchief, shook if briefly, folded it again into a neat triangle, and brushed at each side of his moustache to remove any lingering crumbs. He also, while Lavinia was busy pouring tea, used the handkerchief to dab at cheeks and brow. He was finding it distinctly hot in the room, a heat compounded, thickened, by sweetish odours. Honeyball's nostrils twitched puritanically. Mrs Cuthbertson, he had realized, applied perfumes to her person, and these then became something else, an element in a new compound, mingling with the transpira-tions of her body. His nostrils twitched again, apprehensively. This thought about the perfume was an unusual kind of thought for him, and he was struggling to get it into shape, express it to himself in the careful formal English he generally used in official communiqués, notes and minutes; watching, meanwhile, from his place on the sofa, his slim, unrelaxed back thrust against velvet-textured cushions, his buttocks dangerously deeply ensconced in the yielding stuff of the sofa; watching Lavinia's form in side view as she occupied herself with the tea-things, the clinging material of her dress shaping itself around the voluptuous contours on her body.

Why had she asked him? He had thought at first pleasurably, that it was to plead with him not to recommend Cuthbertson for the take-over. She did not know, of course, that decisions of that kind did not rest with him. He was merely a cog in the Ministry machine, he merely made reports. It was on the basis of many reports, and on general expediency, that the decision, if there was a decision, would be made. He had said nothing of this to Cuthbertson, because it had been Eric's express instruction not to, and in any case he enjoyed the sense of power which prolonging Cuthbertson's anxiety conferred on him. He had been hoping Mrs Cuthbertson would plead with him on her husband's account, then he could have begun the delicate process of bargaining for a rent-free office in the School. If only, tonight, at the party, he could whisper to Eric that it was as good as settled! Then, surely, he too would qualify for a citation . . . But the several allusions, which, in order to give her an opening, he had made, she had ignored or carelessly dismissed. Obvious, then, that she had other ends in view . . . She was turning to him now with his tea. Smiling. Fine figure of a woman, he told himself uneasily. What would Eric have said, how would Eric have managed things?

'Here we are.' Lavinia advanced upon him, bearing the steaming cup. 'Do you mind the music?' she said. 'I can turn it off if you like.'

'Pray don't do anything of the sort,' Honeyball said, raising a slim hand in protest.

'I like a bit of background music,' Lavinia said, rather vaguely. The music so far had not been very suitable. One or two raucous groups, then some negress plangently bewailing her lot. None of it very conducive to the languorous mood she was aiming at. But things were improving now. It was excerpts from *The Desert Song*. Apparently there had been a reissue.

'I didn't hear who the singer was,' she said. 'Did you? It doesn't sound like the tenor who did it on the original one, does it? More nasal somehow. What was his name, do you remember?'

'I'm afraid not, the name escapes me,' Honeyball said. Mrs Cuthbertson was wearing open-work sandals, and he had just noticed, with a distinct shock, that her toenails were painted scarlet, in a highly barbaric manner. She had excellently shaped feet, excellent. The veins rather prominent. Fine figure of a woman. He drank his hot tea with injudicious haste, scalding his mouth slightly. He gasped a little, opening his mouth to let cool air in.

'Takes you back a bit, doesn't it?' Lavinia said, noticing nothing of this. 'My goodness.' She laughed and touched her hair, as if those days still needed living up to. 'Not that I saw the original show, of course.' She laughed again.

Mr Honeyball stared blankly at her for some moments, then with a shaft of insight saw what needed to be said. 'Saw it?' he said. 'I should think not. You weren't born then.' He smiled thinly, pleased with his graceful compliment, worthy, he thought, of Eric himself.

'I wouldn't go quite so far as that,' Lavinia said. She smiled tenderly at Mr Honeyball, and crossed her legs with a certain carelessness. 'Don't forget you're coming to my party tonight,' she said.

'As though I could forget,' Honeyball said, keeping up the tone.

'I did tell you about the masks, didn't I?'

'Yes. I have my costume all prepared.'

'Don't tell me what it is; it's bad luck. No one will know who anybody is, until we all unmask at midnight. You can guess, of course. No harm in guessing.'

'I think it's a marvellous idea,' Mr Honeyball said.

Lavinia raised her head alertly. 'It is Richard Tauber,' she said. 'That is who it is. Beautiful voice, hasn't he?'

'He has indeed,' Mr Honeyball said. 'Very mellow.' He did not care for music of any kind.

'It was Sigmund Romberg who wrote the music. The director

was a man named Fink. I knew all their names at one time. I still think it's the best musical that's ever been. So romantic, you know. I think a good musical should be unashamedly romantic, don't you?' She gave him a meaning look. 'I am very romantic in my outlook,' she said.

'My friend, Eric,' Honeyball said quickly, scenting an opportunity, 'Eric Baines, who you have been kind enough to ask to your party tonight, he is a very romantic person, too. He listens a lot to the music of Gilbert and Sullivan. He is a very fine man, I'm sure you'll like him. He's a real patriot. You'll hardly believe this, but at present he has absolutely nowhere to – '

'I would call that more operetta myself,' Lavinia interposed, rather sharply. She did not really like Mr Honeyball praising another man to her. It showed a generous nature, of course, but he should be promoting his own interests. All the same, this Baines sounded an interesting person.

'Well, the years pass,' she said. 'We can't put the clock back.'

Nothing if not sensitive, Mr Honeyball had noticed the change in Lavinia's tone, the slight note of reproof. She was obviously not ready yet to lend an ear to Eric's predicament. Selfish cow, he thought with a spurt of vindictiveness. A great man like Eric. Cautiously he sought again that vein of gallantry which had seemed so successful. 'The years have wrought no loss to you, dear lady,' he said. From the depths of the sofa he inclined his narrow head with timid courtesy. 'They have given you dignity,' he said, 'without detracting from your bloom.'

Lavinia smiled dreamily at him, in an effort to live up to this. She felt however that things were not really moving to any sort of climax, nothing was coming to a head. Mr Honeyball was constantly defusing things with his elaborate language and old-world courtesy. He was also half-submerged in the sofa, and there seemed no immediate way of getting at him. They might go on like this for the rest of the afternoon.

She surveyed Mr Honeyball thoughtfully. It was shyness, of course. Underneath, she felt sure that he was rearing to go. Interiorly speaking, he was rampant. Look at the way he was sitting, rigid backed, tense, as if coiled for a spring. Like a beast of the jungle, some questing predator. His knees were pressed together, and the creases in his trousers made sharp, fierce lines.

'Milk?' she said, with a peculiar emphasis, leaning towards Mr Honeyball, with the milk-jug poised above his cup. This posture, by allowing the loose dress to fall away in front, revealed the full glory of her upper breasts, which were presented some eighteen inches from Mr Honeyball's eyes, in all their scented, slightly heaving nudity – a devastating effect she was hoping, and one which, in any case, rendered her hospitable question distinctly ambiguous.

Mr Honeyball pressed his back against the sofa. His forehead felt clammy, and the sides of his nose prickled. Overt sexuality in women had always frightened and repelled him. 'Just a little,' he said, looking fixedly at the jug in his hostess's hand. 'Just a drop.' In self-protection, in the evasive energy his mind had to summon to escape from the effulgence and blandishment of that bosom, he recalled the sequence of names his hostess had uttered in connection with *Desert Song*.

'Ironical,' he said, raising his fragile-seeming head in pride and contempt. He was wedged now in the corner of the sofa, so that he felt secure at least from rear or flank attack. He looked beyond Mrs Cuthbertson, at the gold and black stripes on her wallpaper.

'What is?'

'Those names,' he said.

The yearning voice of the sheikh came over to them, full of a desolation far beyond the words it was uttering:

> *One alone, to be my own*
> *I alone to know her caresses*

'What do you mean?' Lavinia said. 'I don't quite see what you mean.' She rose from her place and sat down beside Mr Honeyball on the sofa, thus entrapping him still further in his corner.

> *This would be a wonderful world for me,*
> *If you were mine alone,*

sang the lonely tenor. Lavinia moistened her lips, looking wide-eyed at Mr Honeyball.

'Romberg, Fink,' Mr Honeyball said, and the names were a bitter incantation against the pressure of Lavinia's thigh. He compressed his lips. The skin above his cheek-bones tightened. He shifted, reducing the pressure slightly. 'They write music about the desert and the outdoor life,' he said. 'What do they know about it?'

'Who?' Lavinia was bewildered. 'Who are you talking about?' she said.

'All those people are Jews, you know.' Mr Honeyball was now again very strongly aware of his hostess's musky odour. He said desperately, 'What do they know about camping out and roughing it? Hiking, and biking, all the things that have made this country what it is. What do they know about it?'

'What about Israel?' Lavinia said. 'Plenty of desert and outdoor life there.'

'Impressarios,' Mr Honeyball said, as if he had not heard. 'Do you mean to say you are not aware of it?' He felt for his handkerchief again, and wiped the sides of his nose. 'You should hear Eric on the subject,' he said. 'My friend Eric Baines.' He was moved. His eyes met hers almost with boldness. 'Everywhere,' he said. 'They are everywhere. In all our vital nerve-cells. Do you mean to say you hadn't realized it?'

7

After Cuthbertson's outbreak about clothing, the staff meeting broke up in some disorder. Cuthbertson sat on at his desk, white-faced, staring in front of him, breathing audibly. Bishop got the staff out somehow, mainly by walking to and fro uttering jovial monosyllables and gesturing in a certain way to show that things were for the moment at an end. Mafferty, staying behind in accordance with instructions, heard him ask Cuthbertson in low tones if he felt well enough to carry on, whether he wouldn't like to something or other – exactly what was not clear to him. He saw Cuthbertson shake his head, and heard him say, in a slow voice, 'You know they have a stupefying effect on me.'

He had no further time to speculate about this as the other two now came out of their rather secretive huddle, and he found himself being regarded. Cuthbertson was still white, but he had controlled his breathing.

'It now falls to my lot,' Cuthbertson said, and with the words he sat forward, with a visible increase of energy and control, 'and I must say that I find the whole business distasteful in the extreme, as I say, it now falls to my lot to tell you, Mr Mafferty, that you have been detected in your forgeries and false pretences.'

'Forgeries?' Mafferty, thinking quickly in this crisis, realized that they must have checked his credentials, after all – he had been hoping it had been overlooked.

'To my mind,' Cuthbertson said, 'to play fast and loose with academic standards is one of the most depraved things that a man can possibly do. *Possibly do.*'

'There was no forgery,' Mafferty said, his native insolence rising within him. 'I demand that you take that word back.'

'Demand?' Bishop said. He took a sudden step towards

Mafferty. 'You change your tone,' he said. 'Change your tone when speaking to your Principal, or I'll give you one on the jaw.'

'Just a minute now, Bishop,' Cuthbertson said. 'Don't allow this fellow to get under your skin. A man who obtains a teaching post through false pretences is not worth losing your temper over.'

'I'll wipe that sneer off his face,' Bishop said. 'What he needs is a straight left on the jaw.'

'No false pretences either,' Mafferty said. 'You keep your distance,' he added, looking at Bishop.

'You are an *anguis in herba*,' Bishop said.

'Do you maintain,' Cuthbertson said, 'that you did not claim to be a Cambridge graduate?'

Mafferty considered a moment. Then he said, 'Yes, I do. I said nothing about having a degree, nothing whatever.'

Cuthbertson looked at him. 'As far as I can see, Mr Mafferty,' he said, 'you are a man devoid of principle.'

'Don't talk to me about principles,' Mafferty said. 'What you are doing is selling degrees, and making a good thing out of it.'

'It is only to be expected a person like you would take that tone,' Cuthbertson said and, to Mafferty's fury, an expression of pity had appeared on his face.

'A word to the local newspaper wouldn't do you much good,' Mafferty said.

'The newspapers both national and local have referred to my establishment more than once.' The look of pity was still on Cuthbertson's face. 'They, like you, were prevented by their own baseness from seeing more than the money aspect. As a result of the publicity we had a flood of applications. It really only remains for me to pay you what is proper and ask you to leave. I will give you a week's salary in lieu of notice. What is the person's salary, Bishop?'

'I'm afraid I can't remember off-hand, Donald.' Bishop flushed guiltily.

'Can't remember? Good God, man . . .'

'One hundred and sixty pounds a month,' Mafferty said, 'and little enough it is, in these days of rising prices.'

'I'll take your word for it.' Cuthbertson said, with contempt.

This conversation appeared to have restored him; there was colour in his face now and his manner was much more collected. He took out a cheque book and fountain pen from his inside pocket.

'I will not have you here in a teaching capacity for one moment longer,' he said, writing rapidly. 'The thought of my charges being exposed to the crude mind of a man who has shown an equal lack of regard for qualifications and for truth, quite frankly the thought is shocking.' He tore off the cheque and handed it to Mafferty. 'However,' he said, 'I don't want to be completely heartless. You may attend the ceremony this afternoon for the last time, if you wish.'

'No, thanks,' Mafferty said. He took the cheque that Cuthbertson extended to him. Rage at being bought off in this way, and at the lofty attitude adopted by the trickster Cuthbertson made it for the moment difficult for him to speak. He thrust the cheque hastily into his top pocket. 'If you think,' he said, 'that I regard it as a favour to go and witness all that flummery, then you are mistaken entirely.'

'As you like.'

Mafferty turned, and after an attempt to sneer at Bishop which rage made into a failure, strode from the room. As soon, almost, as he was outside, reaction set in. He felt the need for a cigarette, but realized in the same moment that he hadn't got any. He thought of Cuthbertson's silver cigarette box on his desk. Now would be a good time to get one while they were still jawing in the Committee Room. The work of a moment to extract a couple. He went quickly along the corridor, down a short flight of stairs, on to the longer corridor that led to Cuthbertson's office. Take the lot, he thought. The word 'Principal' had been painted over, leaving the door completely blank, like a cancelling of Cuthbertson's identity. It was not locked. He went swiftly over the thick carpet and reached over the desk for the cigarette box. Haste, however, the apprehension of being surprised there, made his movements clumsy. He caught with the sleeve of his jacket a pile of type-written cards, barely noticed until this moment, stacked at the side of the desk alongside a pile of quarto-sized papers. The cards went here and there across the desk. Mafferty thrust several cigarettes into his pocket, encountering as he did so Said's essay on 'Divorce' which he had thrust there earlier. He gathered the cards together carelessly, without paying particular attention to them. When he glanced at the uppermost document of the other pile, he saw at once from the variously coloured inks and elaborate Gothic script that these were the actual degrees. They were arranged in order, ready to be conferred. Sweating with haste, but unable to resist the vindictive impulse, he mixed them up with a rapid shuffling process. Then Said's essay came again to his mind. As if fate were favouring him, the sheets were almost exactly the same size. Quickly he inserted the loose sheets of the essay among the pile of degree certificates. Then, exhilarated and appalled, he rapidly left the room.

At the end of the corridor he met Cuthbertson and Bishop. He had a vivid impression of their two faces: Cuthbertson's massive, thick-eyebrowed, curiously rigid-looking; Bishop's pink-cheeked, marked by a sort of uncertain joviality as if there were some joke he hadn't quite seen yet. Neither of them spoke, and in a moment he was past.

It was not until he was back home, in his lodgings, that he thought of the cheque. When he did so an exclamation broke from him. Date, sum, signature, all were completely illegible – merely a series of indecipherable scrawls.

'I have always felt,' Lavinia said, 'that you were a person I could rely on.'

She and Mr Honeyball were strolling in the private garden at the back of the house, separated by a high privet hedge from the part used by the students, and Lavinia was contriving as many light collisions as possible in the hope of arousing the slumbering beast in Mr Honeyball.

'I always thought you fair but kind,' she said.

'I always made it my first concern that no regulation of the Ministry should be contravened,' Honeyball said.

'Very right and natural,' observed Lavinia, brushing his flank with her hip.

'At the same time,' Honeyball said, stepping directly aside over the wet grass, 'I do not think I interpret the regulations too narrowly. If for example I come up against a room which is both cloakroom and toilet, I give it credit for being both. Certain colleagues of mine, admittedly men of an older generation, would say it must be one or the other.'

'Not too rigid,' Lavinia agreed, experiencing a slight heaving of the abdomen.

'There must be some latitude of interpretation,' Honeyball said.

Lavinia stopped in her walk and turned to him. She had thought that being out of doors might do something for Mr Honeyball: he had seemed so ill at ease on the sofa. And indeed he looked better now, more relaxed. An open-air man, obviously, she thought, returning to her earlier idea of him, happier in the great open spaces.

'It doesn't do to be *too* flexible,' she said, and looked at him with lips slightly parted.

The rain had stopped now, but there was still a good deal of moisture in the air. The hedges and shrubs in the garden were dark-looking, motionless, as if tensed by their burden of moisture. Somewhere at the end of the garden a blackbird burst into loud song.

Mr Honeyball smiled his narrow, white smile. His moustache stretched with humorous, knowledgeable effect. He was pleased with Lavinia's words of commendation.

'Dear lady,' he said, 'I am so glad that you will be meeting Eric this evening.'

'After hearing so much about him I feel I know him already,' Lavinia said, with some asperity. She was beginning to feel slightly dismayed at the number of times this Eric's name cropped up in Mr Honeyball's conversation.

'He will be able to explain to you, far better than I, some of the things we stand for,' Mr Honeyball said, not noticing her change of tone in the fascination of the topic. 'I hesitate to call them ideals,' he added, giving her a quick glance, then looking away. 'People don't always understand our aims,' he said. 'We are very short of funds, too. You'll hardly believe this, but we haven't even got an office of any sort. To use as a base, you know.'

'That seems a terrible shame,' Lavinia said. 'Why, there are rooms in this house that Donald never uses.'

For a moment Mr Honeyball was unable to believe that she had actually uttered such propitious words. Then, in his elation, he permitted himself the remark that proved his undoing. 'What a marvellously understanding person you are,' he said. 'As well as beautiful.'

'Do you really think so?' Lavinia experienced a quickening of the pulse. He had never said anything so bold, so intimate, before. The moment had come, she felt. She moved two steps nearer and leaned the front of her body lightly against Mr Honeyball. 'I would not refuse you anything,' she said. 'I know the longing that is pent up within you.'

Mr Honeyball was taken completely by surprise. Too late he saw where this was tending. 'Eric,' he said desperately, 'will be glad, will be delighted, to have the opportunity of – '

'Never mind Eric,' Lavinia said. 'I realize your loyalty to your friend, but we must think of ourselves now.' She leaned against him more heavily. Mr Honeyball, caught off balance, clasped his companion loosely behind her elbows, whereupon Lavinia kissed him.

Mr Honeyball released her arms and stepped back. She could read no expression on his face but a sort of vagueness, as if he were cogitating something very remote.

'What a darling man you are,' she said, moving again towards him.

'We can be overlooked,' Mr Honeyball said. 'Anyone glancing through one of those upper windows – '

'True,' Lavinia said. 'How practical. Let's go inside.' Seeing something change in Mr Honeyball's face, she said, 'It only means a few minutes' more delay. Be patient, darling.' In a low voice she began to give him instructions. 'You must use the side entrance,' she said. 'The secretary would see you if you went the front way. Go round the side of the house from here and you will see it, halfway along, a green door. There is a separate staircase to the first floor, when you get to the top of the stairs go straight ahead. My bedroom is the last room on your left. No one will see you.'

'But your husband,' Honeyball said. 'The students.'

'Donald will be in the midst of the Presentation Ceremony by this time. He will be far too busy to think of anything else. And no student ever uses our part of the house. Wait for me in my room. I'll go up the usual way. You'll be there first, I should think, but I won't be far behind you.'

These words fell warmly and precipitously from Lavinia's lips. She regarded Mr Honeyball's narrow serious face, seeming to detect in it an impatience similar to her own. 'I won't keep you waiting long,' she said. 'I promise.'

Mr Honeyball nodded dumbly, completely unnerved by this cannibal eagerness. He could think of no way of disengaging himself. This latter-day Messalina must be at all costs kept well disposed. Everything, the whole future of their operations in the town, depended on the gallantry of his bearing now. He thought briefly of his room, too far away now, almost, for desire or regret, his warm cluttered little room at home, in the house he shared with his sister. Hearing the blackbird's uninterrupted song, he felt as if he had drifted or been wafted somehow into a world totally contrived by people he would not have liked, had he met them.

He forced on to his face what he hoped was an expression of ardent desire. 'Don't be long,' he said – it was his heroic moment. 'Don't be long, darling.'

Mr Adams had had a trying time with the tap. He had begun work with a certain satisfaction, feeling that he had put that brazen secretary in her place, and vindicated the essential decency of the British working man. He had assumed, moreover, on first seeing the dripping tap, that it was a matter merely of a perished washer, which would take no more than five minutes to replace and yet enable him to charge for an hour's labour. The artisan, in his person at least, was not going to be taken advantage of.

So it was with something of an initial glow that he approached the tap. To his annoyance, however – and confirming his general sense of the household's depravity – he found that the tap was loose on its thread; it slipped when he tried to close it off. It was one of those wide-mouthed, swanky taps, typical, he thought of the sort of people who would have a pink and black bathroom. He carried spares of the standard sort, nothing like this. He would have to dismantle the tap partially, and deepen the bottom threads. A fiddling, unrewarding job without aesthetic or technical interest. Mr Adams straightened up, catching sight of himself in the wall mirror as he did so: a bad-tempered-looking man, with scant hair and disproportionately large ears. When we get a more just society, he told himself, no one will be allowed taps like this; there will be the one standard tap for all domestic interiors. No one will ever again be able to assert privilege, wealth, or class distinction through the type of tap they use, or come to that the type of bathroom appurtenances generally. Brothels will be closed down. Mr Adams looked vindictively at the ceiling. They've made it easy too long, he told himself. Their days are numbered.

To his further annoyance he found that he had not brought up a file fine enough for the job. He had to go back to his van to get one. He made a mistake on the way down, took the wrong turning, found himself going further into the interior of the house instead of towards the street, heard from behind one door on the ground floor a tenor voice singing a song that was familiar.

> *Lonely as the desert breeze*
> *I may wander where I please.*

The words of the song continued to reverberate in his mind as he retraced his steps. Even when he was back in the bathroom again, they returned to him from time to time.

The mains tap was high up on the wall at the side of the electric immersion heater, and this caused some return of his resentment. Typical of these people to have their mains tap in such an inaccessible place. No consideration whatever for the people who provide the nation's wealth. Their days were bloody numbered. He had to climb on to the edge of the bath in order to shut the water off, which was a dangerous proceeding. Actionable, he thought. If I slipped off here and did myself a mischief, it would be bloody actionable.

However, some time later, when the job was finished and the tap replaced, Mr Adam's mood lightened. All he had to do now was turn the water on again and check there was no leak. He put a piece of cloth on the edge of the bath so as not to scratch the enamel when he climbed up to reach the mains tap. The words of the song came back to his mind and he began to sing, in a gusty baritone,

One alone to be my own,
One alone to share my caresses.

'Excuse me,' Mafferty said. He had not succeeded in getting back
in time to reach Cuthbertson in his office, but had managed to
reach him just as, accompanied by Bishop, he was making his way
down the last bit of corridor towards the main hall, Bishop was
carrying the certificates with both hands, the cards stacked neatly
on top. Both men were wearing gowns, Bishop's a threadbare
black one, Cuthbertson's black with a scarlet hood.

'What is it?' Cuthbertson said. He looked at Mafferty for a
moment, then the solemn anguish of his face broke suddenly into
a smile. 'I knew he wouldn't be able to keep away,' he said to
Bishop.

'It is about the cheque,' Mafferty said. In the interval,
remembering certain oddities of Cuthbertson's that day and on
former days, and with the evidence of the illegible cheque before
him, he had decided that the Principal was deranged, and needed
to be handled carefully.

'Check?' Cuthbertson said. 'Check what? Everything is in
order. Still, it was a generous impulse. There is some good in him,
you see,' he said to Bishop.

Mafferty looked with fascinated apprehension at the papers in
Bishop's hands. Should he say anything about them? Cuthbertson
might refuse to amend the cheque. If he kept quiet the thing might
sort itself out somehow without his being involved. In any case,
responsibility for it would not be immediately laid at his door.
Once he got the cheque corrected he could be over the hills and far
away.

'He isn't wearing a gown,' Bishop said.

'Not that kind,' Mafferty said. 'I am referring to the cheque – '

'Where is your gown?' Cuthbertson said. 'You can't attend
without a gown.'

'It is in the staff-room,' Mafferty said. 'I'll go and get it.'
Perhaps there would be a chance later, he thought. Urged on by
mingled curiosity and horror, he was not slow to get his gown and
return. Those flocks which have nibbled through countless school
assemblies were still safely grazing as he took his place on the

122

platform, between Beazely and Simpson. Bishop, Dovecot and Binks were on the other side, thus forming Cuthbertson's right flank. The Union Jack, draped over the table, was in vivid contrast to their dark robes. On it, directly in front of Cuthbertson, were the two neat piles, formed by certificates and cards, to which Mafferty's gaze kept returning.

Bach's pastoral music continued to fill the hall with a sort of reassuring gentleness. The students were almost all assembled now. They sat in ranks, facing the platform. Cuthbertson had had a notice put up concerning dress to be worn by students attending the ceremony, and they were all dressed appropriately, in dark suits. The gathering included quite a large number of students who were not actually receiving degrees on this occasion, but hoped, by attending, to impress the Principal with their seriousness. Mafferty glanced sideways at Cuthbertson from time to time. There was something elemental, frightening, about Cuthbertson's face, Mafferty thought. It was possibly the least mobile face he had ever seen. No doubt or reservation or anxiety seemed ever to pass over it. It was a face that had no middle range of emotion. Even during that curious outburst during the staff meeting, Cuthbertson's face had remained passive. He had showed no flicker of expression, either, while making those illegible marks on the cheque . . .

The students sat sedately, directing at the platform their variously pigmented features. What did they make of it all? Uneasy at the fiasco he sensed on the way, worried about his cheque, hoping desperately that he had by some marvellous fluke replaced the cards in the right order, though the odds against this, he knew, must be astronomical, Mafferty fell again to wondering how far the students lent themselves to this deception, how far conniving, how far beglamoured. Probably the same proportion here as elsewhere, the same mix. Knaves and fools . . . Cuthbertson must know the degrees were bogus, and yet, and yet . . . Mafferty could not understand. He was exasperated at the incongruity of it. Here they all were, investing this crudely commercial process with pomp and ceremony. He among the others, sitting in their borrowed robes. Perhaps it was this, the very pointlessness that was the point, transcending all categories of deception. It was pointless not in any philosophical sense of value, but pointless here and now, immediately and self-sufficiently pointless; perhaps this was therefore the thing that had the most point, giving formal notation to the pointlessness, pointlessness before therefore — While he was still struggling amidst these speculations, the music clicked off suddenly. The hall was still. Cuthbertson rose to his feet.

Honeyball was nearly at the top of the stairs when he remembered his brief-case. He had placed it against the sofa when he sat down to have tea. It had remained there, only inches from his left calf, throughout the entire proceedings. Criminally, in his relief at escaping into the open, he had forgotten, he had left it lying there. He stopped dead. My God, he thought, remembering the Contingency Plans, remembering Eric's words. A cold hand closed over his heart. He must go down again, at once. He could not possibly leave the brief-case there a moment longer, risk its being found, possibly opened and examined, by some unauthorized person. The decision, while not lessening his anxiety, brought an immediate rush of relief on the amatory level. As he went softly back down the stairs he tried to persuade himself that what he was experiencing was disappointment, that this was a case of stern duty triumphing over the clamorous demands of the flesh. Only a pleasure deferred, he told himself . . . He felt like a man reprieved. Of course, once he had got the brief-case again in his possession, he would make his way back round to that green door, mount those stairs that led to a rent-free office on the premises . . .

Once more in the garden, he went rapidly round to the front of the house. He had hoped to enter without being noticed, but Miss Naylor saw him from her little office — her window looked out on the front path. She thought it rather peculiar to see him appear from the side all alone like that. He looked nervy too, biting his lip and moving his right arm outwards from his side and back, in a series of stiff little movements. As though he had lost sixpence and found a penny, as she later expressed it to Mrs Garwood. However, she said nothing of all this, merely went to the door of her office and enquired with some hauteur whether she could help him.

'Well, I was just going,' Honeyball said, 'but I've left my briefcase in the sitting-room.' He saw some curiosity on the girl's face and with the instinct of a conspirator, he calmed himself, imposed stillness on his body. He must not behave as if the brief-case were of any particular importance. 'Silly of me,' he said, forcing a smile. 'I thought I'd better . . . No, don't bother to come with me. I know exactly where I left it.' It wasn't there, however. Nor anywhere else in the sitting-room. The tea-things had been cleared away and there was no evidence of recent occupation. For a moment he thought he had mistaken the room, but there was no mistaking the sofa. He was obliged to go back to Miss Naylor's office. 'It isn't there,' he said, making an intense effort to control his anguish. 'My brief-case isn't there. It has gone.'

'Oh dear,' Miss Naylor said. She put her hand up, in this crisis, to pat her hair, and Mr Honeyball, with that particularity which descends on a man in deep misfortune, noticed that her nails were silver. 'I've only been away from the room half an hour,' he said, and swallowed convulsively.

She accompanied him back to the sitting-room and looked in. 'It's been cleared up,' she said.

'Cleared up?'

'Mrs Garwood's been in.'

'Who is Mrs Garwood?' Honeyball said wildly. 'Good God, who is Mrs Garwood?'

'She's the housekeeper. Now, I wonder what she's done with it. She takes things into the kitchen sometimes.'

Mr Honeyball looked at her. He had a terrible desire to raise his voice. Lavinia would be up there waiting. 'It must be found,' he said.

'Sometimes she puts things in the hall,' Miss Naylor said. 'Not the main hall, the little hall at the front entrance. I'd ask her, but I don't know where she'll be. I've known her take things up to the Principal's office; not often, mind. Perhaps we'd better look in the hall first.'

Lavinia was surprised to find that Mr Honeyball was not awaiting her in the bedroom. She wondered briefly if he could have lost his way, but this seemed unlikely, in view of the simplicity of the route. Perhaps, she thought, he had stopped on the way for some reason of his own. The toilet perhaps. To occupy the time while she waited, she slowly and languorously undressed. When she was naked she applied *Mon Trépas*, fairly liberally to various of her zones. Then she put on her black silk nightie. Still no Mr Honeyball. She went to the door, opened it, and looked out down the passage. No sign of life along there. However, as she was about to withdraw her head, she heard a series of slight metallic sounds from the bathroom. She walked quietly along the passage and stood outside the bathroom listening. The door was ajar. She heard a sort of scraping sound, difficult to identify. Then from within a baritone voice was suddenly raised in song:

> *One alone to be be my own*
> *One alone to share my caresses . . .*

Lavinia's face broke into a smile. She pushed the door open further and looked in. 'Hurry up, darling,' she said. The singing stopped abruptly. Mr Honeyball was not at the wash basin, as she had expected. He was standing with feet apart on the edge of the bath, reaching up to something on the wall. She could see his reaching arm, but head and torso were concealed by the immersion heater. As she watched, the arm was slowly lowered. Suddenly Lavinia remembered the dripping tap. Mr Honeyball must have noted it on his way along to her room, and chivalrously stopped, to do what he could in the way of quick repairs. Mistimed, she thought, but a generous gesture. 'Oh, you darling man,' she said. 'Don't bother with that now.'

A sort of coughing noise came from behind the heater. 'What did you say?' Lavinia took three short steps across the bathroom floor. 'How *sweet* of you,' she said. Mr Honeyball's crotch was just about at eye-level and in an impulse of affection Lavinia raised her right hand and gave it a gentle congratulatory squeeze. 'Come on *down* from there,' she was saying, but already in that second of contact, she had experienced a flashing intimation of wrongness, of some dreadful mistake too late to remedy, a realization derived from incongruities only half-registered at the time now suddenly coalescing — the strangeness of Mr Honeyball's singing voice, the absence of polish on his shoes, of crease in the navy-blue trousers. Her sense of having blundered badly was at once confirmed, even as she snatched her hand away, by the convulsive jerk the figure had given at her touch, the desperate slipping of his feet on the edge of the bath.

Appalled, Lavinia stepped back and saw a total stranger, a person in a cloth cap, come sliding into view, clinging to the front of the immersion heater. She watched him scrabble briefly for a hold on its smooth convex surface, then fall with a terrible crash on to the bathroom floor, where he groaned, writhed briefly, then lay still.

'I really am most terribly sorry,' Lavinia said, bending over him in great distress. 'I took you for someone else.'

But Mr Adams was only partially conscious, and quite unable to make any reply.

There was no sign of the brief-case in the hall. It took them a while to find Mrs Garwood, who was Hoovering on the other side of the building. She remembered finding the brief-case, yes. She had put it in the lost property cupboard.

'Where is that?' Honeyball shouted.

'What?'

'Would you mind switching off that machine for a moment?' The muscles behind Honeyball's fragile knee-caps were quivering. 'Where is the lost property cupboard?' he repeated, more quietly.

'In her room.' Mrs Garwood pointed at Miss Naylor. 'Where I puts all the lost property,' she added.

'So it has been in your room all the time?' Honeyball said, turning white-faced to confront Miss Naylor.

The secretary put up one hand to her nape and felt at her back hair. 'Well, we can have a look,' she said. 'No harm in having a look.'

At this moment, from somewhere above them, there came a loud crashing sound.

'What was that, do you think?' Miss Naylor said to Mrs Garwood.

'It sounded like it came from Mr Cuthbertson's side,' Mrs Garwood said.

'Never mind that now,' Honeyball said. 'My brief-case – '

'It'll be that plumber,' Miss Naylor said. 'Throwing things about. They've got no respect for anything.'

'They don't care, do they?' agreed Mrs Garwood.

'My brief-case,' Honeyball said again, reduced by now almost to pleading.

More time was lost in returning to Miss Naylor's office.

However, they found the brief-case there, in the cupboard, and with it once more in his possession, Mr Honeyball though a slight feeling of nausea persisted, felt confidence returning. He said goodbye with no great cordiality to Miss Naylor, and stood for some moments at the front door clutching his brief-case to him. In the stress of searching for it, he had lost count of time and had no idea how many minutes had elapsed since he had parted from Lavinia in the garden. Could he get round to the side of the house, he wondered, begin again, so to speak, at the green door? Perhaps he would be seen going along the front of the house. And could he get into the garden again without going past Miss Naylor's office – a proceeding which would seem strange? He simply did not know the house and grounds well enough to make a proper plan.

It was the arrival of the ambulance that finally decided him to leave. It came down the drive in a swift white rush, and hissed to a halt on the gravel of the forecourt. Two white-clothed men got out and began taking a stretcher from the back. Mr Honeyball made a last attempt to get the thing in perspective. Leaving thus unceremoniously would be a clear dereliction of duty, so much was undeniable. It might to some extent prejudice the prospect of a rent-free office on the premises. On the other hand, if there had been an accident of some kind, people would soon be milling around, the privacy necessary for his encounter with Lavinia would in any case be sacrificed. An ambulance could arguably be considered in the light of *deus ex machina*, something unforeseen, uncontrollable, altering the whole situation, and as it were dissolving previous contracts . . .

Mr Honeyball began to walk briskly across the forecourt away from the house.

'Where's the accident, mate?' one of the ambulance men said to him as he passed.

'I have no idea,' Mr Honeyball said, and he walked away down the drive.

'Mr Jabi Assuan Lavent,' Cuthbertson called in clear tones. 'Bachelor of Arts with first-class honours.' A dark-complexioned man rose from the second row and made his way to the steps at the side of the platform. There was scattered clapping from the ranks of the students, aided by the gowned staff on the platform. Smilingly, Cuthbertson watched as Mr Lavent mounted the steps towards him. 'I admit you,' he said, extending his hand, 'in the name of the authority vested in me.' He shook hands with the new graduate, and handed over the first parchment from his pile. With utmost gravity Mr Lavent returned to his place. There was another burst of clapping.

'Mr Juan Allargon Rodrigues,' Cuthbertson called. The method of distribution had not varied for several years now. He always had the names typed out in order of presentation on separate cards, since the elaborate Gothic script of the degree certificate was extremely difficult to decipher. All he had to do was read out the name and hand over the scroll – these had all been arranged in order by Miss Naylor.

'I admit you in the name of the authority vested in me,' Cuthbertson said, shaking hands with the enormous shaggy Venezuelan who had appeared in answer to his call. The solemnity of the ritual was already taking hold on him. His own sonorous voice, pronouncing the historic formula of admission, the periodic bursts of applause, the vivid colour and perfect regularity of the Union Jack covering the table before him, all contributed to give him a sense of being the instrument of some higher purpose.

'Mr Tien Sieu,' he called. 'Bachelor or Arts with first-class honours.' A diminutive figure in the front row stood up, but made no move to approach the platform.

'Come forward,' Cuthbertson called encouragingly, but the slight, yellow-faced person still made no move, merely stood there at attention. Cuthbertson turned and conferred briefly with Bishop. A faint buzz of comment came from the assembled students.

'What is the matter with him, do you think?' Cuthbertson said anxiously.

'It may prove difficult to get to the root of it,' Bishop muttered. 'His English is weak, to say the least.'

'Will you please step forward and receive your degree,' Cuthbertson said, aiding his meaning by beckoning with the card he was holding. Mr Sieu said something in reply, but his words were completely unintelligible.

'What did he say?' Cuthbertson looked round at his black-gowned staff. He felt the situation slipping out of his control. Was this some kind of demonstration? Little throbs of panic, like twinges of pain, began to assail him. 'Mr Sieu,' he called again. 'Will you please – '

At this moment there was another disturbance. Mr Rodrigues, who had been looking closely at his own certificate, now also stood up. 'No, no, no,' he said loudly. Cuthbertson goggled at him, clutching at the front of the table for support.

Mr Sieu spoke again, still standing to attention.

'What does he say?' Cuthbertson appealed to the students sitting nearby, but they all shook their heads or looked down at their feet. A student on the other side of the room, similar in general appearance to Mr Sieu, stood up and there was an exchange of words in some high-pitched, wavering tongue.

'Excuse please,' this second student said. 'He say, not Bachelor of *Art*, Bachelor of *Science*.'

'Science?' Cuthbertson's feelings of panic increased. He looked down at the certificate, forcing himself to focus on its ornate medieval script. After some moments he saw that it was not made out to Sieu at all, but to a person named Hacaoglu.

'The papers are in the wrong order,' he said aside to Bishop. He looked at the next one, hoping this would be Sieu's, only to find that it was not a certificate at all, but what seemed part of an essay. 'Good God, what is this?' he said. '. . . sophism to anger me,' he read, 'so much Rather than putting it henceforth and to clarify my opinion that the action of committing divorce is neither caused by a woman nor does it affects the church or government. Acts of prostitution, barrenness, quarrels, and impecunious depressments . . .'

He looked up dazed from this to see Rodrigues starting to walk towards the platform, waving his certificate rather menacingly over his head. 'No, no, no,' the Venezuelan shouted. 'Is not my name.'

Mr Lavent was frowning and shaking his head over his certificate. 'Agriculture,' he was saying to those nearest him. 'What means agriculture?'

'Couldn't you collect them in and start again?' Bishop whispered.

Cuthbertson raised hands to his head. Certificates fell from his nerveless grasp and scattered over the table and floor. Members of staff went down on hands and knees to pick them up. Rodrigues had begun to climb the steps to the platform. The strains of 'Sheep May Safely Graze' once more filled the hall. Bishop, with what he himself felt to be commendable presence of mind, had put the record on again.

At this moment two white-coated figures, closely followed by Miss Naylor, entered the hall and after a brief hesitation began to make their way up towards the platform. They did not go round to the steps, however, as their way was blocked by the enormous Rodrigues waving his certificate. Instead they took up positions immediately below the platform. Miss Naylor, standing between them, spoke upwards from here to Cuthbertson, who was obliged by the general hubbub to crouch slightly and crane his head forward in order to make out what she was saying.

'What?' shouted Cuthbertson, looking down at Miss Naylor and at the white coated figures flanking her. 'Accident? What accident?'

Binks, creeping on hands and knees about the platform, had meanwhile picked up a hand-written sheet of paper. 'What on earth is this?' he said to Bishop, who was beside him. He read a few words, with Bishop looking over his shoulder, 'As it has been to my personal intrepidity, divorce is, and is to be one of the most delusive actions in the political phenomena . . . Acts of prostitution, barrenness, quarrels and impecunious depressments . . .'

'I say,' Binks said, 'I've heard that before. It is part of Mafferty's essay. One of his students, I mean.'

'Are you sure?' Bishop stood up suddenly, and looked round the platform, but Mafferty was nowhere to be seen.

'I don't know anything about an accident,' Cuthbertson shouted. He leaned over, looking at the three upturned faces. The white-coated person on the left was speaking, his mouth was moving, but the noise in the hall, and the continuing strains of Bach, drowned the words.

It was at this moment, crouching forward in an unnatural posture, straining to hear, aware of the chaos around him, Degree Day in ruins, his staff scuttling about on hands and knees, that Cuthbertson felt that violent impulse towards freedom and destruction rise again within him, stronger than ever before, taking the form now of terrible mirth, an overmastering urge to break into laughter. This for a moment longer he fought against, unable, however, to prevent a smile from appearing on his face as he gazed down at the trio below him.

'Accident?' he said. 'Good Lord, no.'

'Excuse me, Donald,' Bishop said behind him, 'I think we've found the culprit.'

Smiling broadly, Cuthbertson moved away from this voice, a little way along the platform, then jumped down. Taking no further notice of the ambulance men, he strode to the exit. Outside the door he met his wife, who looked, not agitated exactly – she never looked that – but somewhat flushed.

'Where are the ambulance men?' Lavinia said.

At this the demon mirth climbed with remarkable agility up into Cuthbertson's throat and forced his mouth open. For one moment more, open-mouthed, he regarded his wife's face; then loud, irrepressible sound broke from him. This laughter took the form of four notes, the first three regularly spaced and at more or less the same pitch, the fourth coming after a slight pause and on a high sustained crowing note.

'Inside,' he spluttered. 'They've got a stretcher.' It was all the words he could manage. Crowing with laughter he went rapidly off down the corridor.

Lavinia looked after him for a moment in astonishment. Then she began making her way through the crowd towards the white-coated persons at the far end of the hall. Some familiar music was playing. She had a glimpse of black-gowned figures moving about on the platform apparently in search of something. Mr Bishop and an enormous indignant-looking man were engaged in some sort of altercation at the top of the steps.

Reaching the ambulance men, she explained the situation to them in a few terse words and led the way out of the hall again, upstairs to the bathroom. Mr Adams had recovered consciousness by this time. He was sitting morosely on the floor with his back against the bath. In spite of all that had happened to him he was still wearing his cap, though it had been twisted a little to one side. He objected at first to getting on to the stretcher, but then the crafty thought of compensation came into his mind. He began to groan and grimace, making the most of his injuries.

'Never mind,' Lavinia said, setting his cap straight.

'It'll be a hospitable job, this will,' Mr Adams said. 'What you done constitutes an assault.'

'You are suffering, in your humble way, from the wounds of love,' Lavinia said. 'Let that be your consolation. Handle him carefully,' she said to the ambulance men. 'I won't come down with you, if you don't mind.'

'What did she mean?' the foremost ambulance man said, as they were going along the passage with Mr Adams on the stretcher. 'What did she mean about the wounds of love?'

'This place is a *bordello*,' Mr Adams said, recumbent on the stretcher.

'Come again?'

Mr Adams sighed. No education. That was what was holding the people back. 'A high class knocking-shop,' he said. 'To you.'

'Well,' said the foremost ambulance man, who had not taken much to Mr Adams, 'you have had a knocking about in there, by the look of it.'

'Catering,' Mr Adams said, 'for a wealthy, foreign clientele.'

'What were you doing there then, having a go?' They were going down the stairs now, and the foremost ambulance man turned to wink at his mate behind.

'I was called in to a job,' Mr Adams said with dignity. 'I was standing on the edge of the bath to get at the mains tap when she come in and caught hold of my privates. "Come on down from there," she said. Well, with the shock like, I lost my footing. That nymphomaniac what you just saw, pretending to be all concerned. I couldn't do nothing to defend myself, see, being engaged with the pipes.'

The foremost ambulance man started to laugh suddenly. He laughed so violently that he set his foot wrong on the stairs, and this made him lose his balance. To save himself from falling, he dropped his end of the stretcher and Mr Adams went rolling down to the bottom of the stairs. He was unconscious again when they got to him.

8

It took Bishop some time to restore order in the hall. Finally, however, the certificates were all distributed, though much less formally than had been intended, and the students dispersed, followed by the staff. Bishop was left alone on the platform, looking down at the empty rows of seats. After all that planning and preparation, he thought. The Chief would be heartbroken. He had put a good face on it, of course, adopted a smiling manner, but underneath he would be feeling it deeply. Bishop knew that.

It was all Mafferty's doing. Mafferty had brought this ceremony, which summed up and epitomized everything the School stood for, into chaos and disrepute. Since the discovery of the essay, Bishop had been thinking about Mafferty a good deal. He had remembered passing Mafferty not far from the Principal's office. What had he been doing there? And there was his flight from the hall just a short while ago. Everyone else had stayed to help. But not Mafferty, no. Mafferty had fled, no other word for it. Cowardly of course, like all his kind. There was no longer any doubt in Bishop's mind: Mafferty was the person responsible. Well, he was not going to get away with it. *Nemo me impune lacessit*, Bishop thought, his breast swelling with indignation. What Mafferty needed was a straight left to the jaw.

Looking out over the hall, he thought of the years in which he had served the Chief, their long association. Through thick and thin, he said to himself, and something inside his throat thickened suddenly. I won't let you down, Donald. A friend showed his mettle in time of true need. Donald would be needing him at this very moment. But where was Donald?

He began, logically enough, by looking in the Principal's office, but there was nobody there. Staying only long enough to slip

Donald's little bottle of tranquillizing tablets into his pocket, he went out again into the corridor. Where next? The School lay in silence around him. There were no teachers on the premises now, no students. The thought of Donald wandering unhappily about the building was peculiarly painful to Bishop. He might of course be brooding in his own quarters on the other side of the house. In that case he would have to be left alone. Or perhaps . . . Bishop raised his head and looked up towards the ceiling. Perhaps the chief had taken refuge from the storm of life on the top floor amid storage cupboards and workrooms. It was worth a try, he thought.

However, as he was making his way back along the corridor he heard a mutter of voices, and emerging on to the wide landing at the end found himself confronted by a number of stocky men in overcoats.

'Hullo,' Bishop said. 'Can I be of any assistance?'

The men advanced in a body, one slightly to the fore. They were all smiling now. When they got near enough they all held out hands to be shaken.

'How do you do?' the leader said. 'How is it going?'

'Quite well thanks,' Bishop said. The handshaking took some time and was marked by considerable confusion. After it there was an uncertain pause, during which the smiles of the men dimmed slowly.

'You have come to enroll, I take it,' Bishop said.

'Roll?'

The men looked at one another gravely. There was a brief interchange among them in some foreign tongue. Then the spokesman turned back to Bishop.

'Mr Roll?' he said. 'I am Yanar. This is Tatesh. This one is Oksuz.'

Suddenly Bishop remembered what the chief had said about visiting Turks.

'He over there is Ajikguz,' the spokesman said. 'It means open-eye.' He smiled broadly and all the others smiled too, as if this last named person was a bit of a joke.

'You are the Turkish Delegation,' Bishop said.

'That is right, sir.'

'The Principal is not available for the moment,' Bishop said. 'He was called away on very urgent business. He asked me to show you round the school.'

'Good, Mr Roll. Understood perfect.'

'No, no,' Bishop said. 'I am Bishop. I am the Senior Tutor.'

The whole of the Turkish Delegation nodded at this, except the man whose name meant open-eye. He said something in low tones to the spokesman, who looked tolerantly at Bishop and said, 'Ajikguz English not so good, Mr Roll. It got rusted.'

'No, no,' Bishop said again. 'I'm afraid you've got hold of the wrong – '

'He is Bishop of this School,' the spokesman said reprovingly to Open-eye. 'Mr Roll is Bishop. He is looking after the welfares of the students. That is named pastoral care. All the up-to-date schools and colleges have pastoral care, don't you know that, Osman? Sometimes called Dean, sometimes called Bishop. You better make a note.'

The Turkish Delegation took notebooks and pens from inside pockets and began to write. Bishop thought of making a further attempt to clarify the situation, but the Turkish Delegation was so obviously pleased to have found at this early stage of the visit something to write about, that he decided to postpone things for the moment, and try later on. Besides, the spokesman, Yanar, was obviously a figure of authority among them and Bishop, with thoughts of Asian self-esteem in his mind, did not want the man to lose prestige.

'Well,' he said, when they looked up from their notebooks, 'shall we go this way?'

He led them from class room to class room, explaining the courses offered at the School, doing his best, too, to set out the educational principles which governed them, as he knew that Donald would have wished him to do this. This tour of inspection took a long time because the patient, thick-fingered Turkish Delegation wrote down almost everything he said, breathing audibly as they wrote.

'Well, I hope,' Bishop said, when they were all assembled again on the landing, 'that this visit will prove of some use to you in the – '

'We are all strongly interested,' Yanar said, 'in your langauge laboratory, Mr Roll.'

'That is on the next floor,' Bishop said, glancing at his watch. It was nearly half-past six. He had been engaged with these people for well over an hour. Thoughts of Donald returned to his mind. 'That will have to be our last port of call today, I'm afraid,' he said. He led the way towards the stairs, the bulky Turks falling into single file behind him.

Inside the language laboratory they stood in a group in the middle of the floor, and Bishop was starting to explain the use to which the various equipment was put, when he thought he heard a distant crowing sound of laughter.

'The whole thing,' he said, 'can be monitored by the teacher from this central control panel. But the students in the individual booths – Excuse me.' He went to the door, opened it and looked up and down the corridor. There was no sign of anyone.

'They can work independently,' he said, returning. 'At their own pace. They can check their own responses, you see, go through the drills as often as they like.' Again he heard the laughter. It sounded nearer now. 'They are partitioned off,' he said loudly, 'and besides they have earphones plugged in to the receiver so that nobody disturbs anyone else.'

'Excuse please,' Yanar said. 'I heard one man laughing.'

'No, I don't think so,' Bishop said. 'These are the individual booths, you see.' He began shepherding the Delegation towards the far side of the room, away from the corridor. Open-eye, however, did not accompany them. He had picked up a pair of earphones from the teacher's desk and was regarding them intently.

'But I am sure,' Yanar said. 'It came from outside, in the corridor.'

'Perhaps one of the students,' Bishop said. 'They are a high-spirited lot. They come up here sometimes. To play ping-pong, you know.'

'Ping-pong?'

'Table-tennis.' Bishop had broken out in a gentle perspiration. 'We believe in promoting physical health here,' he said. 'In fact that is one of the principles of the School. We offer the students an all-round education. No aspect of personality is neglected.'

138

'Write it,' Yanar said to the rest of the Delegation. He did not have the look of a man whose mind is completely at rest.

'They can come up here and let off steam,' Bishop said. 'No, no,' he said to Open-eye, who had put on the earphones and was now smiling and moving his head, as if in acknowledgement of sound issuing forth. 'You won't hear anything that way. It is not plugged in.'

He took up the end of the flex attached to the earphones. '*Mens sana in corpore sano*,' he said to Yanar. 'You know the old tag?'

Holding the flex he moved towards the wall where the sockets were. The flex, however, was not long enough by several feet to be plugged in while Open-eye remained in his present position. 'Will you move this way a bit?' Bishop said.

Open-eye, hampered no doubt by the earphones, did not seem to have heard him. He was still nodding and smiling.

'This way,' Bishop said. He gave a tug on the flex, bringing Open-eyes head down a little and obliging him to move a step or two forward.

'Not far enough,' Bishop said.

At this point there was another burst of laughter from outside, unnervingly loud now, on four notes, the last a sustained crowing one.

'All work and no play,' Bishop said, using his free hand to get out a handkerchief and wipe the sides of his neck, 'makes Jack a dull boy. It is the old idea of the Greek gymnasium.'

'Jack?' Yanar said suspiciously. 'The Greeks we do not like.'

'A general term,' Bishop said. He was slowly drawing Open-eye, by means of a series of commanding twitches on the lead, step by step across the room. 'Another couple of feet and we're there,' he said.

'We do not like educational methods of Greeks,' Yanar said. 'That is not the laughter of ping-pong.' He went suddenly to the door, opened it and looked out. 'There was a man,' he said, returning. 'In a black dress. Long, like a *Chorak?*'

'*Chorak?*'

'In my country,' Yanar said, 'only women wear the *chorak*. He went very quick round the corner.'

'One of the students, having a breather,' Bishop said.

Yanar went over and removed the earphones from Open-eye's head. 'Laughing and dressed womanish,' he said to Bishop. 'Is he Greek?'

He said some words sharply in Turkish. The whole Delegation began to regard Bishop with hostility.

'Thank you, Mr Roll,' Yanar said stiffly. 'We are leaving now.'

'Very well,' Bishop said.

They went down the stairs together in silence, and said goodbye in the main entrance hall. The Delegation did not offer to shake hands and it was sadly apparent to Bishop that the visit, though attended with so much note-taking and initial good will, had not been an unqualified success, that the Delegation, in fact, were almost certainly leaving under the impression that the School harboured laughing Greek transvestites. There was nothing he could do about it, however, and besides he was very worried about the Chief, so as soon as the Turks were off the premises he made his way back as quickly as possible to the top floor.

The corridor running past the language laboratory was deserted, but when he reached the point at which this was intersected by another, shorter one, he suddenly saw a gowned figure standing stock still some twenty yards away on his left. Bishop was startled by the figure's absolute stillness, by what seemed some painful distortion of the features, and by the gown –it had not occurred to him that the Chief would still be wearing his gown, and he now understood Yanar's misapprehension.

He advanced some paces and saw that what he had taken for distortion was in fact caused by a fixed smile. The Chief glanced round as if seeking some means of escape and what made this odd was the fact that the smile did not disappear. There was a strong sense of incongruity in Bishop's mind, as he began to move quickly forward, between this smile and the hunted manner in which Donald glanced about him.

'We got everything sorted out, in the end,' Bishop said. 'Everything is all right now, Donald.'

His fingers closed over the little box of pills in his pocket.

Lavinia was standing before the mirror in her room, putting the finishing touches to her costume, taking occasional swigs from a large whisky designed to put her in the party mood. She was now, in appearance and in her own conception of herself, the orgiastic Goddess of Love, whose cult was notorious throughout antiquity for the abandoned behaviour of its devotees. Her costume consisted almost entirely of glass beads. Numerous strings of them fell from neck to waist, attached to a loose neckband of smooth glass. The upper part of her body, beneath the beads, was naked. Her beautiful arms could conceal themselves under the cascading glass or ripple out when she raised them, like a swimmer's limbs emerging from spume. Her large breasts gleamed voluptuously through the bead screen. So that they should tone in better with the pale, opalescent effects of the glass, she had painted her nipples silver. Below the waist she wore silver lamé briefs and a thin snake belt attached, from which strings and strings of glass beads descended to her ankles.

Lavinia surveyed herself in the mirror and was pleased with what she saw. The whole effect was one of shift and glimmer and change. The pale, faintly gleaming droplets of glass glittered and shifted in their own light, and cast light by reflection of the flesh below. This interaction, the glitter from the cut surfaces of glass with the denser, satiny gleam of the skin, made for a glamorous flux of light: when she moved, even slightly, the whole front of her shimmered, glittered. When she walked forwards towards the mirror her smooth heavy thighs bulked nakedly through the beads, with barbaric marmoreal splendour. Her face too, was deeply impressive. She had decided, instead of wearing a mask, to paint a mask on. She had given herself silver lips, cheekbones, eyelids; great black eyebrows going in cruel oriental sweeps to the temple. The face that looked at her now was unrecognizable: magnificent, cruel and strange.

She stood there for some time, delighted with the effect. One of the elements in her pleasure was the fact that Mr Honeyball would be there. Though her feelings towards him had completely changed since the contretemps in the bathroom, she was not averse to reminding him of what he had that day through pusillanimity missed – pusillanimity or some equally inexcusable blundering. She hated a feeble or ineffectual man, and his failure to arrive at her bedroom at the proper time, after she had actually set him on the stairs leading up there, proved him to be one such. Nothing, she felt, could excuse such a failure, nothing but some sort of stroke or seizure experienced by Mr Honeyball in the throes of anticipation and the exertion of climbing the stairs. This had manifestly not happened. Mr Honeyball had simply done a bunk, thus involving her in all that trouble with the plumber.

Such behaviour puts a man Beyond the Pale, Lavinia told her strange, cruel face in the mirror. Its difference from her everyday face renewed her sense of the possibilities of the evening. Mr Honeyball was not the only pebble on the beach after all. She experienced the familiar excitement, unchanged since childhood, of being prepared for a party, for some encounter that might fulminatingly change the course of her whole life. Perhaps tonight was the night. A childlike wonder at her own existence came sweeping over her. Here's to *you*, she thought to herself, taking a swallow of the whisky. Her attention was distracted suddenly by the flickering of the television set in the corner. She had switched it on earlier to watch a beauty competition, but then the nine o'clock news had come on, and it had been so gloomy, so fraught with disaster, that Lavinia had become oppressed, feeling her world threatened, and she had turned the sound down, leaving the announcer mouthing, doing his nightly mime of kindly, concerned uncle. Now, however, there were suddenly pictures of emaciated black people, sitting and lying here and there in a sort of compound. Something to do with the famine, she thought vaguely.

The door of her bedroom opened behind her. Through her mirror she saw her husband enter, neatly dressed as a referee.

'Hello,' she said, with some constraint. 'So here you are. I was wondering where you had got to.' She regarded him with apprehension. Not having seen him since the afternoon, when he had strode away laughing, she had no idea how much he might have discovered since about the injury to the plumber and the events leading up to it. She was half expecting him to upbraid her, but he merely nodded, as if he had been asked to confirm something, then stood in his referee's outfit. 'Have some whisky,' she said.

'No, thank you.' Confronted by this shimmering stranger

whom he knew to be his wife, Cuthbertson was confused. Bishop had insisted on four pills, afterwards accompanying the chief to the door of his room. Knowing the slowing-down effect the pills had on him, Cuthbertson had made a point of changing into his costume at once and had then made his way to his office, where he had spent the intervening time sitting at the desk, looking before him. Stray resolutions had come to him during this time, worthy of inclusion in the file, but he had made no move to write them down. Now, though a little too portly for running, he looked every inch the referee, with his dignified gravity, neatly creased navy blue shorts, white stockings and Royal Corps of Signals blazer. On his feet black plimsolls. He looked a man whose whistle and raised forefinger footballers would obey. His eyes, through the lenses of his glasses, surveyed his wife with a drugged steadiness for some time, then transferred themselves to the silent TV screen. Amid wrecked-looking huts and hovels, within some sort of enclosure, bundles of whitish rags were lying here and there, quite still.

'Is it more bombs?' Cuthbertson said, enunciating with care, and making a slow gesture towards the screen.

'No, it is these people dying of starvation,' Lavinia said. 'They should not show pictures like that, in my opinion. I was beginning to feel quite worried about you,' she added, referring again to his long absence.

'Worried,' Cuthbertson repeated without particular inflection. He had never said anything to Lavinia about his pills, being unwilling that she should know his weakness. 'It looks as though there has been an explosion there,' he said.

'Are you feeling all right?' Lavinia said. 'Have a spot of whisky. I'm having some.' She did not want to risk any differences of view just then, conscious as she was of being in the wrong rather, of having behaved injudiciously that afternoon. Presumably Donald knew nothing much about it as yet, otherwise he would have made some reference. All the same she was uneasily aware that she had not heard the last of the injured plumber, and wished to postpone all reckonings until the morrow, until after her triumphant apotheosis as Goddess of Love. Moreover, she had noted, though preoccupied with her own troubles, the chaos in the hall that afternoon, and had surmised that something, apart from the ambulance men, must have ocurred to disrupt Donald's degree ceremony. These things, she felt instinctively, must be avoided as topics of conversation. 'Put you in the party mood,' she said, pouring herself another large whisky.

'I am not worried,' Cuthbertson said. His lips felt stiff, as if they were not following exactly the intention of his speech.

'I mean me,' Lavina said. 'I was worried.'

'What about?'

'It doesn't matter now.'

Both of them turned, having reached this impasse, to look at the television screen. A woman with enormous eyes and skin stretched tight over the facebones was looking out at them. The camera advanced on this starving face in dream-like motion, gently, soundlessly enlarging it until its suffering filled the screen. Cuthbertson found himself listening for the faint hiss that should have accompanied this, resembling as it did to him a cunning, high-speed process of inflation.

'They ought not to show such pictures,' Lavinia said. 'Those people have a right to privacy.'

She turned back to the mirror and began touching up the silver on her eyelids. Cuthbertson surveyed her glinting back with a sort of cautious curiosity. The sedative was beginning to take its fullest effect now. His tongue felt heavy, and he could not tell whether his mouth was open or not, whether his lips were in contact or had fallen apart.

After some moments his gaze returned helplessly to the television screen. In a drugged silence, like sleepwalkers, figures in whitish robes, some of them hooded, moved slowly against a sort of low wall, or stockade. In the gritless, effortless silence the figures had a less than human immediacy, were only slightly more palpable than shadows. In slow succession Cuthbertson watched forms, faces, receding, advancing ballooning from the baked earth, sinking soundlessly back again. Image followed image in a drifting dance.

Cuthbertson listened again for the pumping, animating hiss. His right hand at his side felt heavy, resisted for some while all efforts to raise it. Succeeding finally, he touched his lower jaw, realized that his mouth was closed, and began to fiddle with the referee's whistle which was slung round his neck on a braided white cord.

'I hope you've remembered your mask,' Lavinia said, turning her face from the mirror to look at him. She had added two tapering silver stripes below the broader black ones that swept from brow to temple.

Cuthbertson nodded again. The glittering shifts in reflection that were taking place all over his wife's body hurt his eyes and confused his mind, after that beautiful slow dance on the screen. With her strangely painted face and myriad glass gleams she did not seem human, not a natural body, but a thing contrived, assembled. There was nothing at all about her that struck him as familiar. She rustled and hissed, and the glass beads were like moving, rippling scales that flexed with light across her body.

He fingered the whistle round his neck. 'The mask is in my pocket,' he heard his own remote and leaden voice enunciate. Glancing sideways he saw a row of dead people on the screen, their bodies stretched out with a sort of voluptuous ease, as if they were sleeping after some feast. The time had come, he realized suddenly, for him to ask his question. 'Do you remember,' he said, 'that week we spent down in Cornwall, before we were married? We had a little cottage above the bay.'

'Yes,' she said, turning her painted face towards him. 'Yes, I remember.'

'I gave you some daffodils.' Cuthbertson said.

'Did you?'

'Why did you cry?'

'Why did I what?'

'Why did you cry?' Cuthbertson said. 'Why did you cry when I gave you the daffodils?'

'I've no idea,' Lavinia said. 'I can't remember anything about any daffodils. It is twenty years ago.'

'Twenty-two,' he said. He stood silent, incredulous, waiting in spite of her words for the explanation. He had been so sure that she would be able to clear the matter up. 'There must have been some reason,' he said. 'You must remember.'

'I cried a lot in those days,' Lavinia said. She drank some

more whisky. 'Put your mask on, let's see the whole ensemble,' she said.

Obediently, still as if in the toils of some net that was subtly, persistently hampering all his moments, slowing him down, Cuthbertson took the rubber mask from the side pocket of his referee's blazer, and put it on. It was a naturalistic mask, flesh-coloured and straight-featured, with black hair swept straight back to blend through a cunning curve of the rubber into Cuthbertson's own hair: a severe, level-browed mask perfectly suited to the persona of a referee.

'That's marvellous,' Lavinia said. 'Except for your height there would be no way of knowing. Unless someone knew you by the knobbles on your knees, but that is not likely, is it?'

'No, not really,' Cuthbertson said. 'There are not many so familiar with my knees as that.'

The mask he was wearing did not cover his ears, but went down almost as far as his chin, being provided with a straight, rather sarcastic aperture for him to speak through with his own voice. This voice sounded heavily vibrant to him at present, and as though occurring only on his own side of the mask like some sort of interior tuning device. Putting his glasses on over the mask, he looked at himself in the mirror and saw a creature in which there was nothing to recognize. The straight-browed mask looked back at him. In spite of the blunting effect of the sedative, Cuthbertson felt an impulse of panic forming somewhere in the depths of his being. For the moment it was no more than discomfort like the first twinge of pain, but he knew it, he recognized it for his companion of the last four weeks of dawns. Now, however, a new element was contained there, intensely alarming, yet at odds with fear: a path, a potential for escape. He stood, motionless, in his mask, senses muted by the drug. It was not the terrible impulse to laughter, though something of that still remained. Deep within him was a movement of energy that warred with fear. While he was striving to apprehend this more clearly, the television screen was suddenly filled with the familiar face of the Prime Minister: the cherubic mouth; the pouches under the eyes defying all the cosmetician's art, badge both of weariness and probity; the smooth, statesmanlike sweeps of silver hair.

'They said he was going to make a statement,' Lavinia said. 'I want to hear something positive for a change, instead of all these people crying woe.'

She swished over to the set with a running gleam of reflections, and turned up the sound.

. . . deny it, they were in time to hear the Prime Minister say, *And I do not confirm it either. It is not so simple as that. There are those on the other side who would deny it out of hand. Or confirm it. But I do not intend to insult your intelligence by simplifying the issues. The issues facing us are too complicated for that. Now you may think I am advocating political opportunism. Playing it by ear. Sitting on our backsides and playing it by ear.*

'Do you mean to say,' Cuthbertson said, 'that you remember nothing about it?'

'Nothing.'

While well aware, the Prime Minister said, *of the dangers and pitfalls, we take an optimisitc view. A qualified view of opi—*
. . . a view of qualified optimism. Our strength, as always, is in the people of these islands. Our people are never better than when their backs are to the wall. But let us be quite clear where our backs are, where the wall is. There are people today who seem in doubt about these vital issues.

'That is what we need,' Lavinia said. 'Some plain speaking.'

'You can't cry and remember nothing,' Cuthbertson said.

'So let me just say this to the British people,' the Prime Minister said. *'We are going to see this through together.'*

'That man,' Lavinia said, 'inspires me with complete – '

At this point the doorbell rang.

'Heavens!' Lavinia said. 'They are starting to arrive. Will you go down and let them in? I'll be down in a minute.'

The first couple were a Pierrot and a Milkmaid. Cuthbertson, wearing a mask, opened the door then backed away a little. This behaviour, in reality governed by fear at seeing the strange masked figures in the vivid light of the overhead porch lamp, was taken by these first guests as a piece of play-acting. They advanced with outlandish gestures, Pierrot doing a sort of short, high-stepping dance sequence, the Milkmaid courtesying and twirling her pink sateen skirt to reveal comical red and white football stockings. Cuthbertson recovered his self-possession, and with a dim sense of rising to the occasion, moved one hand slowly up to his whistle and managed a short blast on it, pointing at the same time with his other hand towards the bar, which went across one corner of the room and had a barman in a maroon jacket behind it. He had no idea who these people were. They laughed, and exclaimed in feigned voices, and moved past him towards the bar.

Lavinia came shimmering down, and music filled the room: some women singing 'Ten Cents a Dance'. Several more people arrived together. Being masked, and not allowed to speak in their own personas, they nearly all announced themselves with some sort of exaggerated or outrageous gesture on entering. Batman stretched his black crêpe membranes and flapped. The pigtailed Chinaman bowed humbly. A mottled toad with an enormous *papier mâché* toad's head actually hopped about the floor. The room became crowded very quickly. Everyone was in the grip of the conspiracy to conceal identity. Those whose masks made drinking difficult contrived to turn away and move their masks briefly in order to drink.

Cuthbertson had retired to a corner where he sat on the floor against the wall, in numb silence, pale knees pressed together. Stray thoughts passed through his mind. Built the place up with my own hands. Saw the possibilities right from the start. No qualifications myself. Regard it as my life's work . . . These customary phrases which normally gave him strength, were rendered dubious by the presence of this loud, garish throng. So difficult was it to believe that he had actually opened his doors to these people, that he began to suspect they had emerged from some sort of breeding-place within the walls. He could open the windows, break the walls . . . This slowly gathering dream of demolition was interrupted by the appearance before him of a hefty female tennis player with a flaxen wig, a simpering mask, and frilly white pants beneath short white pleated skirt. She was carrying a tennis racquet.

'We sporting types should stick together,' this creature said, in a high-pitched obviously falsified voice. 'Do you mind if I sit beside you? If I get out of line you can point to the penalty area, can't you?' She sat down beside Cuthbertson with ostentatious adjustments of her skirt. Her legs were covered with pale hair.

'Who are you?' Cuthbertson said, but the Tennis Player appeared not to hear this. Her mask had a round red patch on each cheek. 'The toad is very good, isn't he?' she said, nodding across the room. The toad was standing near the bar talking to a sheikh, whose face was concealed by the folds of his headdress and by dark glasses. 'Or is it a she, do you think?' the Tennis Player said. 'Difficult to tell, isn't it? I find that very exciting, don't you? Not knowing what sex people are. Awfully good idea, people keeping their masks on till midnight. By the way, have you seen our host?'

With difficulty, with a sense that words were forming like drops, like some sort of condensation, on the inside of his mask, but were not perceptible on the other side, Cuthbertson repeated the word 'host' and leaned forward interrogatively.

'Cuthbertson,' the Tennis Player said. 'Donald Cuthbertson. Do you know what he came as? No, probably not. It was a well-guarded secret.'

Cuthbertson's lips laboured again behind the aperture cut in the mask. 'Referee,' he said.

'I can see that,' the Tennis Player said. 'To tell you the truth, I'm a bit worried about him.'

'It's me,' Cuthbertson said. 'Cuthbertson.' More people entered the room, headed by a tall person in a tin helmet, his face covered by a primitive gas-mask with a respirator like an abbreviated trunk. Behind him was a man with a three-cornered hat, a mask with an eye patch, and a hook at the end of his arm.

'That's right,' the Tennis Player said. 'I take it you don't know what he came as? Noisy in here, isn't it? I'd no idea she'd asked so many.'

'Who are you?' Cuthbertson said, advancing his mask towards the astonishing, unchanging, simpering mask of the other.

'Gorgeous Gussie,' the Tennis Player said. 'Couldn't you tell?'

Before there could be any reply to this, the music, a saxophone rendering of 'Moonlight and Roses', increased suddenly in volume, and several people began to dance.

A shimmering form detached itself from the crowd and stood

before them, the mask of silver and black paint giving her face a cruel fixity and authority. Standing very close to them she raised her arms and swayed slightly, and her whole body glittered and hissed.

'I say,' Gorgeous Gussie said. 'What a marvellous costume. She is not wearing anything but beads.'

'People have got to dance,' the Goddess of Love said. 'It is absolutely compulsory.'

'I have reason to think this is a man,' Cuthbertson said.

'What does that matter?' the Goddess said. 'You two must dance together.'

'Mustn't disappoint our hostess.' Gorgeous Gussie got up, laying her tennis racquet against the wall behind her. 'It *is* Lavinia, isn't it?' she said.

'Not Lavinia, no,' the goddess said, turning away, sharply, with a swish of beads.

Cuthbertson and Gorgeous Gussie moved towards the middle of the floor where a number of couples were dancing. The music had changed to an old-fashioned waltz. Cuthbertson took the large, slightly moist paw of his partner and put an arm round her waist. They began to circle clumsily. The noise in the room was now very loud. A globe-shaped lamp on a stand near the wall began to swivel slowly, flashing alternate rays of red and blue and white across the room. The blare of the saxophone, the noise of voices and laughter, the revolving light, the close proximity of Gorgeous Gussie's thick satiny body and simpering mask – all combined to confuse and distress Cuthbertson, in whom the drug had effected a temporary impairment of the power of judging distances, so that he was continually being startled by the fact that his feet returned to the floor sooner than expected. In addition to this, he was bewildered by the constant flushing and paling of masks and costumes around him, and by the variegated expressions of the masks themselves. At one point he tried to break free, get off the floor, but laughing masks and sad masks and coldly formal masks bobbed around him, blocking every way. The music changed suddenly, quickened. Gorgeous Gussie wiggled her hips and clapped her hands. Her mask kept up a fixed simper at Cuthbertson.

At the far end of the bar, facing towards the dancers, slightly apart from everyone else, the Toad and the Sheikh continued their conversation.

'I'm afraid it was rather a contretemps,' the Toad said. 'Well, perhaps that is overstating it.' His toad's head, made of *papier mâché*, fitted right over his own head, like a helmet, and his voice emerged through the wide but narrow toad's mouth with a curiously muffled effect. 'It was a chapter of accidents, really,' he said, feeling hot and guilty inside his helmet.

Briefly, presenting things in a light as favourable to himself as possible, he gave the Sheikh an outline of the afternoon's events, leading up to his unfortunate failure to consummate things with Lavinia. 'It was the appearance of the ambulance,' he said, raising his mournful toad's face, 'that finally defeated me. It arrived just at the wrong moment.'

The Sheikh regarded him in silence. Dark glasses concealed the upper part of his face, the folds of his headdress the lower. 'For the true man of action,' he said at last, 'there is no such thing as the wrong moment. You appear to me to have bungled the whole business.'

The Toad lowered his head.

'She will be offended, of course,' the Sheikh said. 'However, I do not think the situation is beyond repair. That wounded self-esteem may work in my favour, as a late-comer in the field. Balm to her ego, you know.' The Sheikh smiled, looking across the room at the dancers. 'You have to be a bit of a psychologist, in our business,' he said. 'You have to know what you are doing. For example, which do you think is she, our hostess?'

'I don't know who anyone is,' the Toad said. 'Except you, of course.'

'You haven't been using your eyes. It is Cleopatra, without a doubt. There she is, over there, dancing with the pirate. I've been watching her for some time now. I'll go over in a little while and ask her if she'd like to try my asp for size.' He laughed, and Toad made hollow sounds of laughter too, through his aperture.

'Home-grown,' the Sheikh said. He laughed again, and pushed back the sleeve of his robe to glance at his watch. It was ten forty-five. He felt exhilarated at the thought that he would be striking a blow for the Party, if he were successful with Mrs Cuthbertson, at more or less the same time as Kirby would be planting his bomb. Very fitting, indeed poetic, he thought, if her conquest could coincide exactly with the explosion: diplomacy and terror going hand in hand . . .

'Well,' he said, 'I can't make any favourable recommendations about you in my report, I'm afraid, not on this afternoon's showing. In fact, it would be better not to go into any detail. In that way the people up at Headquarters will not enter it as a black mark against you. You will not emerge with either credit or blame. It is the best I can do for you, I'm afraid. And if I succeed with the lady I will mention you as the introducing agent and go-between.'

'Thank you,' Toad said, with gratitude and humility.

'Well, here's to Cleopatra.' The Sheikh raised his glass. 'The serpent of Old Nile, to quote the bard.'

'And here's to a rent-free office on the premises,' Toad said. He had to raise his mask a little in order to drink.

'Mark her well,' said the Sheikh. 'Dancing and laughing there, tricked out as an Egyptian queen. On such unworthy objects greats causes and movements sometimes depend. We are all in travesty now. But the day is coming, and coming sooner than – '

'Excuse me.'

Turning, they saw a figure in an old-fashioned crash helmet, dark green in colour, fitting closely round the face like a medieval knight's. The face itself was obscured by enormous black goggles.

'What on earth are you?' the Sheikh said.

'Despatch Rider,' this person said. 'First World War. Do you know which is our host?'

He peered through his goggles at the Toad and Sheikh. The lenses were scratched and grainy, so that sight was darkened and blurred by them. He had been in the pub till closing-time, celebrating with Weekes their acquisition of the lease on a house in Stratford-on-Avon, a perfect place, Weekes said, for a School. The noise, and the changing effects of the light, and the large quantity of beer he had drunk, confused his mind and vision, gave him a sense of being involved in some strange, clamorous, irridescent twilight, full of flickering shapes and forms. He was unwilling, however, to remove the goggles, partly because of the edict against it, mainly because he didn't know where Bishop was, nor what he looked like, and couldn't risk being recognized until he had a chance of running Cuthbertson to earth, and getting his cheque changed. They needed every penny now, to get the School going.

'I'm afraid not, old boy,' the Sheikh said. 'You'll have to wait for the witching hour.'

He nodded and moved away. The Despatch Rider watched him thread his way through the dancers to the opposite side of the room. Here the goggles lost track of him in the murk. All the same there had been a similarity in build and gait to Cuthbertson, and the Despatch Rider was not convinced that this was not his host. When he looked round, the Toad was no longer in evidence, but a female tennis player with a flaxen wig and a grotesquely simpering mask, who was carrying what looked like a Guiness away from the bar, knocked lightly against him and said, 'Oops! Steady the Buffs.'

The Tennis Player had abandoned his falsetto and now spoke in a man's voice which, although slightly muffled by the mask, was familiar. 'Cheers!' he said. 'Excuse me.' He turned aside a little, pulled his mask outwards from his face, and tilted his glass to drink. Mafferty, hampered by the goggles, did not succeed in identifying him during this process.

'Do you know who our host is?' Mafferty said. 'It isn't you, is it?'

' 'Fraid not,' the Tennis Player said. 'I'm trying to find him myself.' He drank again *'Bassum est optimum,'* he said. 'Beer is best.'

Suddenly Mafferty knew who the Tennis Player was, and extreme caution descended on him, in spite of his drunkenness.

'You won't go far wrong on beer,' the Tennis Player said. 'Your voice sounds familiar. You're not a member of staff, by any chance?'

'No, no,' Mafferty said, in an artificially deep voice. 'I am a friend of Mrs Cuthbertson.'

'Oh. She's not wearing anything under those beads you know.'

'Really.' Mrs Cuthbertson must be the one in strings of beads then, with the black and silver face. If he kept a watch on her, perhaps she would lead him to her husband. Mafferty peered down at his watch: it was gone eleven. He had an hour before the unmasking. It was essential he should escape detection until then. His eye fell on the figure of a referee, sitting against the far wall. 'I only know one person here,' he said, 'and that is Mr Mafferty. He told me he was coming as a referee.'

He nodded at the Tennis Player and allowed himself to drift away through the crowd.

'I didn't get a real chance to thank you,' the Sheikh said to Cleopatra, 'for asking me to your party tonight.'

'Not at all,' Cleopatra said. 'I am delighted you were able to come.' She was wearing a tall headdress and a rather in-human, bird-like mask with a prominent, beaky nose-piece.

'Kind of you to say so,' the Sheikh said. 'I hope you won't take it amiss if I say something personal to you?'

'Go ahead,' Cleopatra said.

'Let me just say this,' the Sheikh said. He had decided on a bold frontal approach. 'Your presence here has made all the difference to me. I am not normally a sociable man. You will not find me in the centre of a crowd. By nature I am solitary. But when I looked across and saw you . . . I knew at once who you were . . .'

Cleopatra threw back her head and laughed, on a deep baying note.

'I am the Principal,' Cuthbertson said. Returning to his corner after the dance he had found himself face to face with a person resembling a very old woman, corpulent, and with extremely untidy hair.

'I told her and no mistake,' this person said. 'I don't mince my words, not when it is a matter of principle. I could only listen to the radio when she said so. She brought it to the Home with her, you see.'

The mask that Cuthbertson looked out on from his own referee's mask was plump-cheeked, wrinkled and shrunken round in the mouth, marked by sagging, drooping skin everywhere. In the soft folds round the eyes there were little white spots.

'That is a marvellously life-like mask,' Cuthbertson said. He still found difficulty in forming and uttering words, though the full effects of the sedative were wearing off now, and he was experiencing a return of tension, of that same conflict of impulses which had earlier sent him wandering around the school. 'I congratulate you on that mask,' he said slowly.

'Mask?' Mrs Mercer said. 'This is my face, and my eyes as blue as when I was a girl. My waist was no bigger than that.' She held up two plump, speckled hands making an unsteady hoop with forefingers and thumbs. 'You could of spanned it,' she said.

'Really?' Cuthbertson said. 'This is my house, you know,' he added, after a pause. 'I am the Principal of this place.'

Mrs Mercer's head, declining in a dozing sort of way towards her black velvet bosom, was arrested at a certain downward point and jerked up again. 'Some people can lay no claim to beauty, past or present,' she said. Since arriving at the party she had spent her time sitting on the floor alongside the bar, drinking rum and peppermint, exchanging occasional remarks with the barman, who had kept her glass replenished. Now, however, with intoxication, her delight at the radio situation could no longer be contained, and she had taken to wandering around telling people about it.

'Yes,' Cuthbertson said, 'I am the Principal.' A desire to confide in this elderly, trustworthy person was growing within him. 'I built the place up with my own hands, actually,' he said. 'I saw the possibilities right from the start. The place was a ruin when I first saw it. It lies adjacent to open country behind, you know, and the open country was taking over. You will hardly believe this, but one of the first things I saw on my initial tour of inspection was a large brown rat. It sat up on its back legs and looked at me.'

'Mask indeed,' Mrs Mercer said. 'Saucy!' She gave Cuthbertson's bare knee a slap. 'My legs is still as good as they ever was. In shape, but there is the veins, of course.'

'Of course, of course,' Cuthbertson said, eager to keep the conversation going. 'The fact is,' he added, 'I never had any qualifications myself, and it was a source of great regret to me as I grew older. I saw in this place an opportunity of giving people what I myself had missed. It had to be commercially viable, of course. I believe in the profit motive. Drake believed in the profit

155

motive. Hawkins believed in the profit motive. Frobisher believed in the profit motive.'

'You've got a nice place here,' Mrs Mercer said.

'I have worked hard over the years.' Cuthbertson looked emotionally at Mrs Mercer through his mask. 'Striving to build something of permanent value. An institution to be proud of. Commercially viable, but with standards, rigorous standards. And I think I succeeded. Over the years.'

'All them years,' Mrs Mercer said. 'All them years, then this afternoon her radio blew up. She misused the volume.'

'Now something has gone wrong,' Cuthbertson said. 'Badly wrong.' He advanced his mask earnestly towards her. 'Something has got in,' he said.

Mrs Mercer's head drooped again, was again raised abruptly. Her hair, which under the combined stresses of joy, alcohol and conversation had finally escaped from all control, fell around her face, partially obscuring it. 'Just this evening,' she said. 'She came and asked me if she could listen to the six o'clock news. She came and asked me. After all them years, it was vouchsafed to me. God was good to a lonely old woman.' She looked up triumphantly through her hair. 'I told her to go and fuck herself,' she said.

The whisky that Lavinia had drunk before the party, combined with the whisky she had drunk since, and the exhilaration of causing a stir with her costume, had excited her spirits and inclined her to amorous speculations about some of her guests, particularly that friend of Mr Honeyball's, whom he had praised so highly to her. She had made several attempts to seek him out, and was at the moment extricating herself from a conversation with a man in the costume of an old-fashioned anarchist, whom she had thought might be Baines until a certain mumbling habit with his plosives had betrayed him as Mr Benny, her teacher in the evening pottery class of the previous winter, of whom she had at one time entertained some hopes, until she had discovered that he lived with another man on terms of domestic intimacy. She had invited them both to her party to show there were no ill-feelings, but it was definitely not with a person of that sort that she wanted to spend time talking that evening.

She was moving away from the Anarchist when a person in a dark green crash helmet and huge black goggles drew near her and said, 'What a marvellous costume. So daring.'

'Thank you,' Lavinia said. 'You look like some kind of beetle.'

'Despatch Rider. First World War.' Mafferty had made several trips to the bar, in between efforts to identify Cuthbertson, and was now finding balance something of a problem – the upper part of his body tended to waver from the vertical even when his feet, as now, were carefully planted and at rest. With a confused recollection that his hostess was a goddess of some kind, he said, 'I have come to worship at your shrine.'

Lavinia smiled and shimmered and her beads hissed. This man was drunk, his costume was ridiculous, he was not tall enough for Mr Baines. She took a step or two away, and Mafferty, seeing her form recede into glimmering mists called after her, 'Is this your consort?' Lavinia looked over her shoulder, and nodded, and Mafferty said to the Anarchist, 'There is something I wanted to ask you about, Mr Cuthbertson.'

The Anarchist had a very elaborate mask, going right up over his face and head, bald and domed on top and with a great spade-shaped libertarian beard below. He nodded at Mafferty's words, but said nothing.

'It is about the cheque,' Mafferty said, enunciating with care. 'The cheque that you gave me this afternoon. It is difficult to read.'

The Anarchist again nodded his imposing head.

'In fact it is impossible.' Mafferty peered forward through his goggles. 'It is illegible,' he said, wanting to drive the point home.

'P—p—perhaps I was drunk,' the Anarchist said. 'Or am. Or p—p—possibly you are, or were. Or m—m—maybe we b—b—both – '

'You are not Cuthbertson,' Mafferty said loudly. He had a sudden desire to bash the Anarchist in the centre of his mask, cave his false features in.

Suppressing his violent impulse, he turned away. He was in time to see, quite close beside him, the bright form of Lavinia and a tall figure in Bedouin dress whom he recognized as the person he had spoken to earlier. They moved away together across the room. For some moments they were still visible, over the heads of dancers and talking groups, then they disappeared and Mafferty surmised that they must have crouched or sat down together against the wall. His early suspicion that the Arab was Cuthbertson returned to him. Man and wife, he thought dizzily. Snatching a brief *tête à tête* in the midst of the throng. He began to make his way, very carefully, towards the point at which they had disappeared from view, peering right and left through his goggles at the fixed expressions of the masks which moved in the process of dancing, and changed with the changing light, but registered nothing that naked faces did. He would have liked to take off his goggles; it would have been like returning to the upper air, but he could not be sure that Bishop was not somewhere on the look-out for just such a move. He moved with precarious equilibrium towards the place where Goddess and consort had sunk down below sight.

Before he could make it, however, he found himself accosted by a very old, stout lady with a mass of gingerish brown hair largely obscuring her face. His vision darkened by the goggles, he was at first under the impression that she was wearing a mask of ingenious make, but then he detected movement of eyes and lashes, and a gleam of moisture – apparently an overplus from the eye – caught in one of the shallow folds of her left cheek.

'Excuse me, dearie,' this person said. 'Do you know where the toilet is?'

'There's one just off the main hall,' Mafferty said. 'It's the way you came in, actually.' He pointed over the heads of people to the door. 'Go straight across the hall,' he said. 'You'll see the door facing you.' In the midst of saying this he saw the Goddess and the Bedouin, having apparently worked their way along the wall, leaving by that very door. 'That's the way I'm going myself,' he said. He made an attempt to move forward, but the old lady did not give way.

'Marvellous, isn't it?' she said. 'All the costumes.' Her head declined slightly, as if she were dozing, and was arrested with something of a jerk. 'I don't know when I've enjoyed a party more,' she said. 'Drink in abundance and a very pleasant class of person. When I was a girl, of course . . .' She shook the hair out of her eyes and reared up her head suddenly to stare him in the face. 'What are *you* supposed to be?' she said.

'Despatch Rider. World War One,' Mafferty said.

'Mask,' the old lady said. 'He asked me if I was wearing a mask. Sauce, I said to him. Saucy! They was often saying things like that. Well if you had listened to everything they said . . .'

'Excuse me,' Mafferty said, trying to edge past. There couldn't be much more than half an hour left now.

'Not like some,' the old lady said. 'But I told her today. It was vouchsafed to me.'

She raised both hands and parted the hair from her face, which bore an expression of tranquil contentment. 'I told her to go and fuck herself,' she said. 'I must go to the toilet.'

'This way,' Mafferty said, seizing his opportunity. 'I'm going in that direction myself.'

'Referee, eh?' Bishop said. 'You are an *anguis in herba*. Not only masquerading as a B.A. Cantab, but it was you who disrupted the degree ceremony this afternoon, wasn't it? It was you who disarranged the Chief's papers. Do you realize that you have driven the Principal to the verge of a breakdown? A man whose shoes you are not worthy to – '

Cuthbertson looked steadily through his eye-holes at the simpering mask of the Tennis Player.

'I don't know what you're talking about,' he said.

'Don't attempt to deny it, I saw you coming away from the Principal's office.'

'Principal's office?'

'Don't prevaricate with me,' Bishop said, grinding his teeth. 'You inserted sheets of gibberish among the degree certificates.'

'All my life,' the Sheikh said, 'I have had an ideal of womanhood, but I had given up all hope of realizing it in this earthly existence.' His voice throbbed with an excitement that gave accents of absolute sincerity to his words. It was eleven-ten: only five minutes to go. 'Until tonight,' he said. It was an historic moment: the first bomb to be detonated by the Party in his area. And at the precise moment of the explosion here he was, getting on to the right terms with a potential benefactress. 'Until tonight,' he repeated, looking at the strangely painted glistening face of his companion.

They were sitting half-way up the hall stairs, holding hands. The hall light was on and they could see each other by it, though not very clearly. Lavinia's black stripes merged into the dimness, her silver one glowed phosphorescently. The Sheikh had taken off his dark glasses.

'I had grown reconciled,' he said, smiling sadly, 'never to finding it. I had come to terms with my solitude.'

'There were others,' Lavinia said. 'There must have been others.' For the first time in her life the language she was uttering and hearing corresponded to her sense of reality and fitness. She was enthralled. 'Others to console you on the way,' she said, looking at the large face framed by the Arab headdress.

'I won't deny it,' the Sheikh said. 'I am flesh and blood, after all. I have the usual instincts and appetites.' He began to describe sexy little circles with his forefinger in Lavinia's soft palm. 'But they were only makeshifts, Lavinia,' he said.

Lavinia rubbed the side of her naked thigh against his gown. 'It is natural in a man,' she said. She raised herself on her haunches and moved two steps higher up. 'Only to be expected,' she said.

'In my soul I was always lonely, even desolate,' the Sheikh said, moving up in his turn.

'Lonely as the desert breeze,' Lavinia said smiling phosphorescently. 'You are dressed the part.' She moved up two more steps.

'I had this impalpable ideal,' the Sheikh said, moving up after her. He placed his right hand on Lavinia's lower ribs, below the beads. 'As I say, I had despaired of ever finding her.' Acting on his own initiative, he moved up two stairs. 'Until tonight,' he said.

'Across a crowded room,' Lavinia said, humping herself up after him. They were near the top of the stairs now. The Sheikh replaced his hand, but higher up and more to the front, taking the weight of Lavinia's left breast.

'Just a look,' Lavinia said, feeling an access of alertness in her silver nipples, 'and although the need of the occasion intervened — '

'One knew — '

'Beyond any doubt — '

'The years fell away — '

'All the hopes and fears – '

They both moved up two steps, and this bought them to the landing.

'Couldn't we steal away for a while?' the Sheikh said. 'It's a bit on the public side here.'

As if to lend emphasis to his words, a little old lady went tottering drunkenly across the floor of the hall below them, presumably in search of the lavatory.

'Couldn't we?' the Sheikh said, leaning towards her. One minute and a half to go. A pity he couldn't have been penetrating Lavinia at the moment of the explosion, but coincidences like that are too exquisite for gross mortals . . .

'Why not?' Lavinia said. 'No one will miss – '

'Excuse me,' a voice said from below them, and looking away from each other down into the dimness they saw a figure in a high round helmet with a glassy gleam where his face should have been, slowly mounting the stairs towards them.

'I'm sorry to disturb you,' the figure said, pausing about halfway up and clinging to the banister.

'What the hell do you want?' the Sheikh said.

'It's about the cheque.'

'Cheque? What cheque?'

'It is absolutely illegible,' Mafferty said.

'I don't know what you're talking about.'

Mafferty removed his goggles. Unhampered by them, he was now able to see that the Arab was a complete stranger.

'Sorry,' he said.

He turned and began cautiously to descend the stairs again.

'That is Mr Mafferty, a member of staff,' Lavinia said.

The Sheikh glanced at his watch again: it was 11.15. Now, now, very now, he thought. To quote the bard. In this obscure corner history was being –

There was a sudden deafening explosion from somewhere at the front of the house, followed at once by the more prolonged, multitudinous sound of shattering glass. The house shuddered briefly and the hall light went out. There were some seconds of complete silence. Then they heard confused shouts from the room below.

'Bloody hell,' Baines said. He stood up abruptly. He knew at once what must have happened. That fool Kirby had made a mistake. He remembered his earlier feelings of uneasiness, of misgiving: those restless eyes, that unconvincing doggedness of manner. Kirby had mixed up the streets. Or he had panicked and, remembering the divided counsels up at Headquarters, had planted his bomb outside the first building that looked institutional . . .

'There must have been an accident,' he said, with an instinct of subterfuge, to Lavinia. 'You'd better phone for an ambulance. Some of those people sound hurt.'

Downstairs, after the first shock, the guests had begun to call out and blunder about in the darkness, except for the Toad and Captain Hook, who had been standing near the wall talking about butterflies when the explosion occurred, and who were now lying stunned on the floor. They were trodden on by various people trying to find a way out. This was not easy, as the bomb had blown in some of the brick-work, and a low pile of rubble was partially blocking the doorway. People stumbled against these stones, bruising and cutting shins and knees. The air was filled with acrid dust. Maid Marian crouched in a corner, whimpering steadily.

A few of the guests, not many, tore off their masks. The darkness was confused by the flaring of matches here and there. These random and shortlived flares, held chest-high while they lasted, cast a weirdly transfiguring glow over faces and masks alike as they peered this way and that, questioning for more light, or a means of escape.

'Keep still,' the Tennis Player shouted. He had produced a cigarette lighter which burned with a long slender jet of flame, and he was holding it up in a shaking hand. His grotesquely simpering mask turned from side to side, in an attempt to dominate the company, quell the panic. 'Now listen carefully to me,' he said. Catching a mouthful of dust, he began coughing violently.

At this point the Referee stepped forward into the wavering light. His mask surveyed the wreckage of the room, the disordered revellers, with an unchanging expression of probity and fair play.

'You've made your bid,' he said, in a vibrant, exalted tone. 'You've done your worst, and you have failed. I am the Principal.'

A woman said, in a tone of wonder, 'My face is bleeding.'

'Don't interrupt me,' the Referee said loudly. 'I am the Principal. Not content with subversive activities of every kind, tonight you have deliberately tried to wreck the place. I have known for a long time that this was pending, but I did not know from which quarter the attack would come. My Senior Tutor was unable to help me, though an able and experienced administrator.'

'Is it really you, Donald?' the Tennis Player said.

'Stand back,' Cuthbertson said.

'Excuse me,' an elderly female voice said, from the darkness beyond the hall doorway. 'I was in the toilet. What was that bang?'

'You fools,' Cuthbertson said. 'This place is indestructible. You can never destroy the spirit of a place like this. It will go on and on and on.'

He regarded the glimmering masks and faces. In the unsteady light they were turned to him mutely, expressive of melancholy, lechery, bewilderment, mirth, all silenced by this rhetoric, all subject to the authority of his voice and manner. The blood beat in his temples. His voice took on the triumphant surge of power.

'I will rebuild,' he said. 'Not only that. I will expand. *Expand*. The logic of the situation demands expansion. Schools up and down the country, with staff conservatively dressed, and properly qualified, sworn to preserve standards. A mighty network of schools. Myself at the heart. Drake believed in expansion. Hawkins believed in expansion. Commercially viable of course, but with standards, rigorous standards. It is what made this country great.'

Available in Norton Paperback Fiction

Brad Barkley	*Money, Love*
Andrea Barrett	*Ship Fever*
	The Voyage of the Narwhal
Rick Bass	*The Watch*
Charles Baxter	*A Relative Stranger*
	Shadow Play
Simone de Beauvoir	*The Mandarins*
	She Came to Stay
Thomas Beller	*The Sleep-Over Artist*
Wendy Brenner	*Large Animals in Everyday Life*
Anthony Burgess	*A Clockwork Orange*
	The Wanting Seed
Mary Clyde	*Survival Rates*
Stephen Dobyns	*The Wrestler's Cruel Study*
Jack Driscoll	*Lucky Man, Lucky Woman*
Leslie Epstein	*King of the Jews*
	Ice Fire Water
Montserrat Fontes	*First Confession*
Leon Forrest	*Divine Days*
Paula Fox	*Desperate Characters*
	A Servant's Tale
	The Widow's Children
Carol De Chellis Hill	*Henry James' Midnight Song*
Linda Hogan	*Power*
Janette Turner Hospital	*Dislocations*
	Oyster
Siri Hustvedt	*The Blindfold*
Hester Kaplan	*The Edge of Marriage*
Starling Lawrence	*Legacies*
Bernard MacLaverty	*Cal*
	Grace Notes
Lydia Minatoya	*The Strangeness of Beauty*
John Nichols	*The Sterile Cuckoo*
	The Wizard of Loneliness
Roy Parvin	*In the Snow Forest*
Jean Rhys	*Good Morning, Midnight*
	Wide Sargasso Sea
Israel Rosenfield	*Freud's Megalomania*
Josh Russell	*Yellow Jack*